"Get out of my house!" shouted a raspy voice.
"Get out of my house!"

A hard bumping sound was heard from the stairway. The
bumping grew louder and louder, faster and faster.

"This way," whispered Gina. Her heart was pounding as
she pulled Carrie toward the window. With all her strength,
she pushed upward on the window frame, but it was stuck
as though glued into place.

"Break it!" cried Carrie, but Gina turned around and
bolted to the front door instead. Without so much as a
backward look, she flung open the wooden door and leaped
across the porch. Carrie was close on her heels as they
fled.

"That was the ghost!" cried Carrie. "I told you there was
a ghost."

*But Gina didn't believe in ghosts. She couldn't believe in
ghosts. Because she was the camp's director and couldn't
afford to be afraid. . . .*

Books by Linda Gondosch

The Best Bet Gazette
The Witches of Hopper Street
Camp Kickapoo

Available from MINSTREL BOOKS

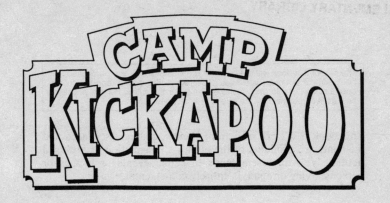

CAMP KICKAPOO

LINDA GONDOSCH

Illustrated by Patricia Henderson Lincoln

A MINSTREL® BOOK

PUBLISHED BY POCKET BOOKS

New York   London   Toronto   Sydney   Tokyo   Singapore

A Minstrel Book published by
POCKET BOOKS, a division of Simon & Schuster Inc.
1230 Avenue of the Americas, New York, NY 10020

Text copyright © 1993 by Linda Gondosch
Illustrations copyright © 1993 by Patricia Henderson Lincoln

Reprinted by arrangement with Lodestar Books,
an affiliate of Dutton Children's Books,
a division of Penguin Books USA Inc.

ISBN: 0-671-75371-1

First Minstrel Books printing July 1995

10 9 8 7 6 5 4 3 2 1

A MINSTREL BOOK and colophon are registered trademarks
of Simon & Schuster Inc.

Front cover illustration by Dan Burr

Printed in the U.S.A.

TO MY FRIEND, MICHELE STEGMAN,
FOR ALL THE ENCOURAGEMENT SHE HAS
GIVEN THROUGH THE YEARS

CONTENTS

1 SPY OF THE UPSTAIRS BEDROOM   1

2 TIFFANY THE TERRIBLE   14

3 UNDERGROUND TREASURE BOX   26

4 A VANISHING ACT   40

5 THE SECRET SUITCASE   53

6 A MYSTERIOUS MESSAGE   67

7 THE KNOCK ON THE CABIN DOOR   81

8 FIREPLACE MYSTERY   98

SPY OF THE
UPSTAIRS BEDROOM

"There won't be enough time for all the things I want to do this summer," Gina told Carrie as they ate bananas at the picnic table. She swept her hair from her sweaty forehead.

"My list is already a mile long," said Carrie. She held out her list for Gina to see.

Hunt for Fossils
Go Hiking
Build Clubhouse in Woods
Swing on Vine Over Creek
Catch Grasshoppers
Paint Pictures
Make Banana Splits and Eat Them (one every day)

"Not bad," said Gina, "but you forgot all about our camp. Remember the camp we had last summer?"

"Camp Kickapoo? Where we got all the kids together and taught them camp songs? I remember," said Carrie. "And I remember how Richard threw a bucket of water on

1

our tent in the middle of the night and stuck a thistle in the end of my sneaker too."

"Your brother doesn't have to know a thing about our camp," said Gina. "We'll keep it a secret. *Top* secret." She picked up an apple core from the table and flipped it into one of the barrels at the end of the patio. "Bull's-eye."

"I don't care how careful we are. My beanbrain brother will find us."

"Beanbrain Richard will not find us," said Gina. "We'll lock him in his closet."

"Or we could tie him to the birch tree and blindfold him." They giggled together just thinking about it, although they knew they would never do it. Richard was impossible to tie down. He could untie any knot, blindfolded or not.

Carrie eyed the barrels. "Say, do you think we could ask your mom for those barrels? They'd make good bumper boats down on the creek. Better than that dumb canoe we had last year."

"I doubt it. She says she's going to plant flowers in them."

"Wow. What a waste." Carrie chewed the last bite of banana as she thought. "They'd make good basketball hoops too. Here, watch me shoot this banana peel." She pulled back her arm and aimed the banana peel straight for the nearest barrel. She stopped in midair as both barrels began to totter back and forth, faster and faster, until they toppled onto their sides and rolled down the slope from the patio. They gained speed as they reached the middle of the yard. One barrel bumped into the birch tree, spun around like a wobbly top, and continued its zigzag trip through the yard. Going full speed, the barrels flew off the back edge of the lawn and plunged a few feet into the weeds and underbrush beyond.

Jed Jawaski dizzily emerged from a barrel, straightened his glasses, and blinked up at Gina and Carrie as they bounded across the yard. "Ow, my head! I feel like a busted bowling ball."

"You look like a—"

"Don't say it, Carrie." Jed rocked his head with both hands.

"Spying on us again!" cried Gina. "Can't you ever mind your own business?"

"Where's Richard?" Carrie stared at the other barrel with a look of horror on her face. "He's probably dead!"

"Richard!" Jed scrambled out of his barrel as fast as he could. "Richard, are you all right?" He stumbled through the underbrush, grabbed the bottom end of the other barrel, and dumped his friend out onto the ground.

Richard sprawled in the leaves, lifeless, his mouth hanging open. Jed shook him. "We never should have done this. I knew it. I told him so. Richard!"

"Quit worrying. He's not dead," said Gina. She pulled a squirt gun from her back pocket and squirted Carrie's brother in the mouth.

Richard's eyes flew open. He coughed and spit out the water. "Hey, cut that out!"

"We're getting tired of being spied on," said Gina. "We can't go anywhere without you two hanging around like a couple of monkeys."

3

Richard grabbed a low-hanging branch and began swinging back and forth, scratching his side with his other hand. "Ooo ooo ooo, aah aah aah," he grunted.

"See what I get for a brother?" Carrie told Gina. "Why couldn't I have a nice, intelligent little brother? Why did I get this THING, this . . . this creature that escaped from the zoo?"

Richard dropped to the ground and scrambled up the bank to Carrie. He stood on tiptoe and put his nose one inch away from hers. "And don't you be calling me Beanbrain ever again and trying to throw banana peels on my head. What do you think I am, a garbage can?"

"You smell like one, Beanbrain," answered Carrie. "Come on, Gina. Let's go over to my house. Let's get away from the THINGS."

"Hey, what about Camp Kickapoo?" asked Jed.

"Camp Kickapoo, spit in your shoe, muddy meatballs, and grasshopper stew," sang Richard, remembering last year's camp song.

Gina slapped her forehead. "You guys can't come to our camp. No ignoramus boys allowed."

"Good. That means we can come," said Richard. "We're not ignoramus boys. Right, Jed? We're smart boys. Very smart." Richard gave Jed a high five.

"I'm a genius," said Jed. "Got an A in math."

Gina laughed. "Yeah, and I'm George Washington's mother. Listen, I'm the camp director here, and I say who's coming and who isn't. And you guys are definitely not coming."

"But I have a bird talk I could give," persisted Richard. "My ostrich talk I gave in science class. You'll love it. Come on, Jed. Let's get the tent." He ran around the house, and Jed chased after him. They disappeared down the long driveway that ran into the end of Clark Avenue.

"They don't hear very well, do they?" asked Carrie.

"Their ears are full of beans."

"You never know where the THINGS are going to pop up," Carrie said. "Last night, Richard sneaked into my room walking like Frankenstein's monster. He pointed a flashlight under his chin, and his face lit up. It almost made my hair frizz."

Gina looked across her wide yard, past her grandmother's rose garden, over to the woods beyond. "Well, we sure kept our plans top secret, didn't we?"

"Well, who would have ever thought the THINGS would be hiding in the barrels?"

"There is one person who must *never* find out about our camp," said Gina.

"Who?"

"Tiffany. She'd ruin everything."

Two months earlier, Gina's mother had remarried, and Gina had unexpectedly found herself with a six-year-old sister named Tiffany and a thirteen-year-old brother named Dwayne. She wasn't sure which was worse, an older brother who grumbled and grouched and locked himself in his bedroom or a chatterbox sister who asked a trillion questions and buzzed around her like a pesky mosquito.

"Yeah, she would, wouldn't she? How about Edie? Let's invite her," suggested Carrie.

6

"She's gone. Myrtle Beach." Gina tried to think of someone else to invite to Camp Kickapoo.

Carrie jumped up. "Uh oh. We're not going to have a camp at all if we don't get my tent."

"That's okay. Let Richard have your tent. We'll use—" Gina stopped when she remembered that her mother had thrown away her tent during spring cleaning. "Oh no! I don't have a tent anymore. Yours is the only one around."

"If you think I'm sleeping in a tent with Richard, you're crazy. He snores like a bear," said Carrie.

Gina thought a moment. "I have an idea!" She sprang to her feet and grabbed Carrie's elbow. "You and I can camp out in the cabin." She pointed to the century-old log cabin that stood almost hidden from view in the woods beyond her yard.

"Oh, I don't know," said Carrie. Although she tried to act casual, her voice revealed her sudden anxiety.

"Oh, come on," urged Gina. "We could clean it out and make a real nice place for ourselves. No ignoramus boys allowed. They get the crummy tent. We get the cabin. How's that?"

"That's not what I'm worried about," said Carrie. "What about—"

"The ghost?" Gina laughed. "Carrie, I've told you a million times there is no ghost in that cabin. That's just a stupid old story."

"Yes, there is! I refuse to sleep in a haunted cabin. Absolutely no way."

But Gina was quickly becoming intrigued with the idea of camping overnight in the cabin that stood abandoned in the woods. "We could fix it up and turn it into our own private clubhouse. Just for us. Come on."

Carrie shook her head vigorously. "No! There's got to be someone around here who has a tent. Now, think."

"Come on, Carrie. It couldn't hurt to go look." Gina walked down the sloping lawn toward the woods and motioned for Carrie to follow.

"No! I said NO!"

"Come on. The spooky old ghost isn't going to gobble you up."

Carrie took a deep breath and let it out slowly. "Why do you get me into these things?" she muttered under her breath. She reluctantly followed Gina across the yard and into the woods. "I'm waiting outside." They took the path through the grove of maple trees.

The log cabin seemed harmless enough. It stood in a clearing overgrown with weeds, wildflowers, and blackberry bushes—remnants of a garden long ago. Gina climbed the two crumbling stone steps to the front porch that stretched across the south side of the cabin. After peering through two dirty windows, she opened the front door and walked inside. Carrie changed her mind about waiting outside by herself and, like a shadow, followed Gina in.

Directly in front of them was a stairway with a hand-hewn railing that led to two upstairs bedrooms. To the left was the main room with a stone fireplace from floor to ceiling. To the right was the kitchen with handmade cabinets, battered with age and use, still fastened to the log walls.

8

"I wonder which room the ghost lives in," whispered Carrie. She stood directly behind Gina and dug her fingers deep into Gina's shoulders as she peered around her into the main room.

"There is no ghost," said Gina. "I wish you'd quit talking like that." Carrie's fears flowed from her fingertips into Gina. "And let go of my shoulder. You're killing me."

Gina blew on the dusty stair railing and coughed as the dust billowed upward. "Let's get some dustcloths and a bucket of soap and water. It's kind of grimy in here."

"Look at all these spiderwebs," said Carrie.

"So what? We'll get a dust mop."

"There are mice in here!" Carrie pointed to the mouse droppings on the floor.

"We'll get a mouse trap."

Carrie held onto the stair railing as if her life depended on it. "This place gives me the creeps," she muttered. "I don't know why, but it feels as though somebody's watching us." She looked back over her shoulder. "Am I crazy, or what?"

"You're crazy," said Gina. They dashed up the stairs and poked their heads into the two bedrooms at the top. In the bedroom on the left the sun poured through the hazy windowpane onto a wooden table and chair, the only pieces of furniture in the house. A straw broom leaned against a closet door. As they came into the room, they noticed crayons, bottles of paint, and drawings of people and animals strewn across the table.

"Who do you suppose drew these scribbly things?" asked Gina. "Looks like something Kevin might draw, doesn't it?" Kevin had been in Gina's art class in school.

Carrie examined the pictures carefully and finally shrugged. "I don't know."

"Well, somebody's been making himself at home out here in my cabin," said Gina as they clumped back down the stairs to the main room below. They carried the pictures and the broom with them. "This is our property, you know. I ought to tell Mom about this."

"Maybe the ghost likes to draw," said Carrie.

"The ghost artist." Gina laughed. She decided not to tell her mother just yet. After all, her mother would never let them spend the night in the cabin with a mad artist loose in the woods. She decided the safest move was simply to lock the cabin door.

Carrie began to sweep spiderwebs from the ceiling while Gina printed a sign on the back of one of the pictures with a red crayon:

```
+-----------------------------+
|                             |
|         PRIVATE             |
|        PROPERTY             |
|                             |
|            NO               |
|     IGNORAMOUS BOYS         |
|         ALLOWED             |
|                             |
+-----------------------------+
```

She found a nail protruding from the front door and pressed the sign onto the nail. "There, that should do it.

"Hey, let's build a fire," she said as she stepped back inside. "We can build our very own fire in this fireplace. Isn't this fun?" Gina took a sheet of paper with a sketch of a butterfly, crumpled it, and threw it into the ashes. She looked around for matches and was surprised to find a matchbook on the mantel.

Carrie hesitated. "We're going to get into trouble."

"Oh, you worry too much. Worrywart Carrie." Gina checked to see that the chimney damper was open, struck a match to the paper wad in the fireplace, and watched as the paper poofed into flame. "Do you know how many campfires I've made in Scouts? I'm an expert. Go see if you can find some sticks outside, okay?" She wadded more pictures, threw them into the fire, and watched as the orange flames grew taller. The pictures slowly curled into shriveled gray snakes.

"I really think we—"

"Shhh!" Gina suddenly jerked her head to the left, eyes down, finger across her lips.

"What's the—"

"Listen!" Gina pointed to the ceiling. Somebody crossed the bedroom above, moving toward the stairway.

"Let me out of here," muttered Carrie. She turned toward the front door but stopped as the upstairs visitor started down the creaking stairway.

"Get out of my house!" shouted a raspy voice. "GET OUT OF MY HOUSE!" A hard bumping sound was heard from the stairway, not coming closer, but not going away either. The bumping grew louder and louder, faster and faster.

11

"This way," whispered Gina. Her heart was pounding three times faster than the strange sound coming from the top of the stairs as she pulled Carrie toward the window. With all her strength, she pushed upward on the window frame, but it was stuck as though glued in place.

"Break it!" cried Carrie, but Gina turned around and bolted to the front door instead. Without so much as a backward look, she flung open the wooden door and leaped across the porch. Carrie was close on her heels as they fled across the clearing and down the path to Gina's yard. They rushed up the slope to the patio and tried to pull the sliding glass door open, but it was locked.

"Open the door!" cried Gina. Her new stepsister, Tiffany, walked to the door and stood there smiling. "Open up!" Tiffany shrugged and held up her hands. They were covered with finger paints.

Gina and Carrie were about to run around to the front of the house when they saw Jed emerge from the woods. He walked with a long stick and poked at the ground.

"Get out of there, Jed," yelled Gina. "There's somebody back in the cabin."

"Who?" asked Jed, looking behind him.

"The ghost, that's who!" cried Carrie. "I told you there was a ghost."

Jed spun around. "The ghost of the cabin?"

"Wait a minute," said Gina, her eyes narrowing as she studied Jed. Her fear drained away and was replaced with exasperation. "That was *you,* wasn't it?" She stood with her hands on her hips. "That was you upstairs in the cabin. Spying on us again. Right?"

Jed's mouth dropped open. "Huh?"

Gina pointed to Jed's walking stick. "Is that what you pounded on the stairs? You just about scared us to death."

"What are you talking about?"

"As if you didn't know," said Gina. "Jed the Master Spy." She started toward Jed, but he turned and ran from the yard. "Don't ever scare us again," she yelled after him.

"You're wrong," said Carrie, catching up with Gina. "That wasn't Jed we heard. It didn't sound like him at all."

"Yes it was," insisted Gina. "I'd know Jed's voice anywhere."

"It sounded more like someone with a really bad case of laryngitis," said Carrie.

"It was Jed. I'll prove it," said Gina. "Come on back to the cabin with me. I bet you a dollar we won't find anything. The master spy of the upstairs bedroom has gone home. Come on."

"No, that's okay. You go," said Carrie.

"All right, I will." Gina ran down the slope and into the woods.

TIFFANY THE TERRIBLE

"Hi! Anybody home?" hollered Gina as she stood just inside the cabin door. Nobody answered. "Richard, are you here? Come out, come out, wherever you are." She searched the entire cabin but found no sign of life. Even the fire in the fireplace had died. She quietly closed the door behind her and walked back home.

Grandma was watching her favorite game show on TV. Gina sat down on the floor and asked herself for the hundredth time, What good is a stepsister if she's not the same age as me? She studied Tiffany as the six-year-old played on the floor next to the coffee table. Why couldn't she have gotten an eleven-year-old stepsister instead of a baby like Tiffany?

"Mom, Tiffany's into my Barbie stuff again," Gina said. Her mother was busy in the kitchen pulling dishes from the dishwasher. She came to the doorway. "You haven't played with your dolls for months, Gina. I didn't think you would mind."

"I do mind," said Gina. "Last week she sprayed hair spray all over them. It took me three days to scrub it off."

"You've got to learn to share, Gina. That's not so hard, is it?"

How could her mother be so cheerful? Life had once been so pleasantly simple. But not anymore. Once there had been just the three of them—Gina, Mom, and Grandma. It had been so perfect. Why did things have to change?

Tiffany held out a doll and a miniature wedding gown. "Can you put this dress on for me?" she asked. Gina took the doll and slipped the wedding gown over its head.

"Hurry up," said Tiffany.

Gina maneuvered the slender doll arms into the sleeves and fastened the tiny snaps on the back of the dress. Tiffany reached for the doll and thrust it into the driver's seat of a pink plastic car. She raced the car around the coffee table and slammed it into the rocking chair. Barbie fell onto the floor, face down.

"Barbie can't get married now," announced Tiffany. "She broke her nose. She's got to go to the hospital." She held Barbie out to Gina. "Can you get this dress off? Hurry up."

"What's your big hurry, anyway?" said Gina. "I'm busy."

"Why are you busy?" asked Tiffany.

"I have things to do."

"What things to do?" persisted Tiffany.

"I'm flying to London for dinner with a gorgeous rock star," Gina responded under her breath. As she walked out of the room, she noticed that all of her doll clothes were strewn across the sofa. The wooden doll cabinet her uncle had made for her several Christmases ago was on its side with one door broken and hanging from a loose hinge.

15

"I can't get this dress off," said Tiffany. She pulled at the wedding gown.

Gina spun around. "Here. Give me the doll." She unsnapped the wedding gown and pulled it off. It was better to help her new sister than to have Barbie's wedding gown torn. "Make sure you put all these clothes back just like I had them, okay? That means hung up on hangers in the cabinet." Gina could tell Tiffany wasn't listening. She was too busy searching for a hospital outfit for Barbie.

Gina picked up her radio. She turned it on full blast and ran up the stairs to her bedroom, passing Dwayne, who was coming down. Her stepbrother wore his usual frown and pretended not to see her as he passed by. It was a good thing Dwayne didn't talk much. That way she didn't have to talk to him.

Gina closed her door and lay down on her bed. She punched all the radio stations and stopped when she found her favorite song. With a shiver, she glanced at the aquarium on the floor next to her desk. Tiffany's three-foot snake, Ozzie, was curled around a branch inside the glass box. He flicked his black tongue at her. She set her radio on the aquarium lid and jumped back onto her bed.

She closed her eyes and thought about her predicament. She couldn't get a nice little sister who liked cuddly kittens. No, she had to get Tiffany, who liked slithering, tongue-flicking reptiles. She couldn't get an older brother who looked like a rock star. No, she had to get grumpy Dwayne who had pimples and grunted instead of talked.

And there was one other problem. Now that Tiffany slept in the spare bed, Gina couldn't invite her best friend for a sleepover. She smiled. Of course, that didn't matter now. She and Carrie could spend the night in the cabin in the woods.

She opened her journal—the one she had begun in fifth grade—and wrote:

Dwayne the Pain has a nervous tic in his eyelid. His eyelid jumps around like a pogo stick. Weird. Tiffany the Terrible almost ripped Barbie's wedding gown today. I'll be buying my own wedding gown soon. I have decided to marry Kevin after all and move away from here. Even though his nose is humongous. My nose is pretty big too. We'll just have kids with jumbo noses.

She turned the page and discovered scribbly pictures made with a red crayon. She turned three more pages before Tiffany's artwork ended. Wonderful, thought Gina. Tiffany's taken over my room. Now she's taken over my journal. She snapped the book shut and stuffed it under her pillow.

"Dinnertime!" called Mom.

Gina ran down the steps and almost collided with Dwayne in the downstairs hallway. Silent Dwayne. Maybe he had been born on an alien planet and didn't know English yet. She took her place at the table, between her grandmother and Tiffany. She was beginning to get used to six people squeezed around the kitchen table.

She looked over at John, her new father, and smiled. He smiled back and winked. John's smile stretched from one side of his face to the other. She liked John. He liked to tell silly jokes and then laugh at them until everyone else laughed too. She was glad her mother had married him. If only Terrible Tiffany and Dorky Dwayne had not been a part of the package deal.

"Ouch!" Gina jumped up and pulled Barbie out from under her.

Tiffany scowled. "Hey, you sat on Barbie! Don't you know this is General Hospital?" she said as she patted Gina's chair.

"This is my chair," said Gina. She picked up Barbie and put her on the floor. Clyde, Gina's white cat, came over and sniffed the doll.

"You probably killed Barbie!" said Tiffany.

"Yeah, and now Clyde's going to eat her for dinner. Barbecued Barbie." Tiffany's hands flew to her mouth.

"It's all right," said Gina's mother as she joined them at the table. "Clyde isn't going to eat your doll." She smiled at Tiffany.

"Let's not worry about Barbie right now," said John patiently. "Let's say grace, shall we?" He bowed his head and began to say the blessing.

Gina bowed her head and closed her eyes. She opened one eye halfway and looked at Dwayne. Even with his eyes closed, his right eyelid kept hopping around. Gina saw Tiffany's chubby hand slowly reach for the bowl of grapes. She turned and stared at her as menacingly as she could. Tiffany smiled slyly. Gina had a great urge to say Get out of my house! just as the voice in the cabin had done a few hours earlier. Instead, she squeezed her eyes shut and tried to pretend that Tiffany wasn't there.

"I hope the mashed potatoes aren't too lumpy," apolo-

gized Gina's grandmother as she passed the bowl to John. Grandma had lived with them ever since Gina could remember.

"The mashed potatoes are delicious," said John. Gina knew he would say that no matter how bad the potatoes were. No wonder her mother had married him. He was a very agreeable man, always smiling, always saying how wonderful everything was. Even lumpy potatoes. John and her mother were right for each other. Her mother worried about everything, and John didn't worry about much of anything.

"Please pass the grapes," said Tiffany.

"Is that all you ever eat?" asked Gina.

"Have some potatoes," suggested her mother.

"No thanks. I want grapes. I like grapes," insisted Tiffany. She piled grapes onto her plate.

"Maybe you'll turn into one," whispered Gina.

"Gina, watch your manners," said her mother.

Gina twirled her fork in her potatoes. "Say, Mom, you know the old cabin out in the woods? It sure is a great place to play."

"I know. I used to play in there myself when I was your age. But it really ought to be closed up. I'm afraid vagrants are going to break in one of these days."

"A couple of drifters once did," said Grandma. "Remember those two fellows passing through town last year? Or was that two years ago?"

"There's a lock on the door now," said Gina's father. "I installed one a couple of weeks ago. No one can get in."

With a shiver of fear, Gina thought back to the moment

when she and Carrie had opened the unlocked cabin door. Someone had gotten in. She decided to say nothing.

"I used to play in that house almost every day way back before any of you were born," said Grandma with a hint of pride in her voice. "Back when someone was living in the old place."

"Who lived there, Grandma?" asked Gina.

"Their name was Owens. I used to go to school with Sophie Owens every morning. I'd stop by her house and we'd walk together to school." Grandma smiled and shook her head. "What a long time ago that was. Poor old Sophie."

"What happened to Sophie?" asked Tiffany.

"Her family packed up and moved away."

"Where to?" asked Tiffany.

"Out to Oklahoma I think it was. Oh, how I missed Sophie!"

"Did you miss her like I miss Sarah?" asked Tiffany. Sarah was Tiffany's friend from Lakeville, the town where she used to live before her father married Gina's mother.

Grandma patted Tiffany's hand. "Yes indeed, I missed her like you miss Sarah. That Sophie. She was a wild one, always in trouble with the teacher, always getting spankings from her mama, always playing tricks on her brothers and sisters. But we sure had fun, Sophie and me."

"She sounds dreadful," said Gina's mother.

"Oh, she wasn't bad," said Grandma, "just chock-full of mischief."

"Is there really a ghost in the cabin?" Gina decided her grandmother would know the answer if anyone would.

Grandma looked startled and then laughed. "Well, not that I know of! Why in the world would you ask a question like that?"

"Carrie says there's a ghost in the cabin."

"That's just a silly story," said Gina's mother.

"Who lived there after that Owens family left?" asked John.

"Some young couple," answered Grandma. "I don't recall their name."

"Someone told me a groundhog got into the cabin once and died in there," said Gina's mother.

"One did," said Grandma. "Of course that was after the house was empty. Nobody's lived in the old Owens place for years. It was such a nice house too. Sophie's mama used to be so proud of her garden. I remember the day Sophie dressed up like a scarecrow, stood by a pole, and spooked her brothers when they came into the garden. She jumped out at them, and they all took off running." Grandma chuckled.

"Why did the Owenses leave?" asked Tiffany.

"Times were bad," said Grandma, "and Sophie's daddy found work out West. I remember Sophie had four brothers and sisters, and she was only allowed to take one toy with her when she left for Oklahoma. That was all they had room for."

"Which one did she take?" asked Tiffany.

"Good gracious, I can't remember. That was an awful long time ago, you know. Sixty years ago." Sixty years seemed like forever to Gina.

"How old are you, Grandma?" asked Tiffany.

"A hundred and forty-nine." Grandma winked at Gina.

"Wow, you're old!" said Tiffany.

John went to the stove to get the coffeepot. "I used to have a Cub Scout troop that held meetings in a log cabin back in Lakeville. Remember that, Dwayne?" Dwayne nodded, glancing up briefly. His mouth was full of food. "We camped out in our cabin one time too. Remember?" Dwayne gave a short grunt.

"Gee, that's just what we want to do," said Gina. "We're planning our camp, Carrie and me, just like the one we had last year. But this year we want to camp in the cabin. The cabin would be so much nicer than a leaky old tent, don't you think? Carrie and I could camp out in the cabin, and Richard and Jed could use their tent."

"Oh, boy! I want to go camping too," said Tiffany. "Can I come too?"

Gina turned around to face Tiffany. "No, not you, Tiffany. You're too little for Camp Kickapoo."

"No, I'm not. Can I camp out with Gina?" she asked her parents.

From the expression on her mother's face, Gina knew what the answer would be. Her mother always said no when anything seemed too dangerous. If only Tiffany had kept quiet. Her mother might have said yes to Gina and her friends camping. But if Tiffany came, suddenly it was too risky. Why had she mentioned the camping trip in front of her sister?

"Nobody's camping in that—" her mother began.

23

"My goodness, I remember when you and all your girlfriends used to stay overnight in the cabin," Grandma said to Gina's mother.

With a look of exasperation, Gina's mother replied, "Maybe so, but that was years ago, Mother."

"I remember how you came home one morning covered in mud," Grandma continued. "I thought you'd slept in a mud puddle." She laughed. "You girls had more fun in that cabin."

"Mother!"

Gina tried to picture her mother as a young girl, her mother playing in a mud puddle. It wasn't easy.

"A camp-out in the woods does sound like fun," agreed John. "Want me to stay there with you?"

A stricken look crossed Gina's face. "No thanks! Whoever heard of a father coming to Camp Kickapoo? We can take care of ourselves. Honest."

"Me too. I want to go to Camp Kickapoo too," insisted Tiffany.

Gina bit her lower lip. Her plans were falling apart. She looked at Grandma and pleaded silently for help. For some reason, Grandma always seemed to straighten things out.

"Oh, why don't you let them go?" Grandma said. "They'll have a good time."

"We'll be real careful, Mom," said Gina. "I promise."

"Yeah, real careful," echoed Tiffany. "I want to go!"

"Tiffany can come too. I'll take good care of her."

Gina's mother sighed. "If you promise to lock the cabin door, then okay. Go ahead. But please be careful. And Gina, you have to watch Tiffany every single minute, do you understand?"

At that moment, Gina knew that Tiffany would be tagging along with her forever, no matter where she went. To school. To the park. To Carrie's. She had just become a full-time baby-sitter, without pay. At least Dwayne hadn't asked to come. He was too busy eating and grunting.

"Thanks!" Gina smiled at Grandma and then rose to leave the table.

She thought of explaining what a problem Tiffany would be at Camp Kickapoo but decided against it. She had gotten permission to use the cabin and figured she'd better not say anything to make her mother change her mind. Tiffany would simply have to be tolerated. Maybe if she tried really hard, she could pretend Tiffany was invisible.

As Gina passed through the kitchen doorway, she overheard her mother say something and Dwayne argue back. She didn't wait to see if the argument was about Dwayne's long hair, Dwayne's dirty shoes, or Dwayne's sloppy eating habits. It was usually about one of those three subjects, and Gina wasn't interested.

Gina was halfway through the living room when she felt a tug on her sleeve. It was Tiffany.

"Are we going to see a real ghost?"

Goose bumps popped up on Gina's arms.

"Of course not."

"Can I bring Ozzie? Please? Are we going to sleep in the cabin? Is there a dead groundhog in there? Do I have to bring my toothbrush? When do we go?"

UNDERGROUND
TREASURE BOX

Gina went upstairs to her room and spent the rest of the evening preparing for camp. She planned activities and made a list of all the supplies she would need. It was no easy chore since most of the time Tiffany sat in the corner singing "Old MacDonald Had a Farm" at the top of her voice and stacking dominoes as high as she could. Every time they fell over, she laughed like a crazy person and stacked them all back up again. Gina cranked up her radio to drown out her sister's singing.

"Don't ever, ever, ever look in my suitcase," said Tiffany after she had investigated the insides of her suitcase and closed the lid.

"What did you say?" Gina turned her radio down a bit.

"Don't ever look in my suitcase," repeated Tiffany.

"I wasn't planning on it. What do you keep in there, a crocodile?"

Tiffany didn't answer. She twisted her mouth into a tight little knot as she turned the key in the suitcase lock. Out of the corner of her eye, Gina watched as her sister lifted the aquarium lid and buried the key in the pebbles at the bottom. Her snake didn't move.

Tiffany climbed into bed. "Turn off the radio," she called.

"No."

Tiffany threw her stuffed tiger at the radio, knocking it over, but Gina's favorite song kept playing. Gina grabbed the tiger and tossed it back to Tiffany.

The bedroom door burst open, and Dwayne stood in the doorway with a book in his hand. "Hey, shut the radio off, huh?"

From the angry look on his face, Gina thought it might be smart to turn her radio off after all. She turned the knob until it clicked. "Out of my room, Pain." Dwayne left.

"This is *my* room too," said Tiffany. "Isn't it?"

"Of course, Tiffany." Gina closed her eyes.

Ten minutes later, her grandmother came in to say good night. Grandma was late tonight, and Tiffany had already fallen asleep. "I brought you a little present," Grandma whispered as she handed Gina something wrapped in pale yellow tissue paper.

Gina pulled the paper loose and gazed at an Indian necklace made from multicolored beads and tiny brown nuts. She slipped it over her head.

"Thanks so much, Grandma. Now I'm all set for Camp Kickapoo."

"I bought it from a Hopi Indian on my trip to the Grand Canyon," said Grandma. "I figured you'd like it. I got one for Tiffany too."

Gina hugged her grandmother. "You're the best grandma in the whole world."

"Even if I am one hundred and forty-nine years old?"

"You're not that old," said Gina.

"No, but I'll be seventy-five on Thursday."

Seventy-five on Thursday. Gina decided then and there that she would get her grandmother the most wonderful birthday present that she could buy. But earlier, she had checked her piggy bank and had found forty-two cents. What could she buy for forty-two cents? Not much. Maybe she could make something. Maybe all the Kickapoo campers could make something stupendous for her grandmother's seventy-fifth birthday.

Tiffany rolled over, and her stuffed tiger fell to the floor. Grandma picked it up and placed it back beside the sleeping child.

"Grandma," said Gina. "Promise you'll never leave me?"

Grandma sat down in the chair next to her bed and took Gina's hand in hers. "Why would I ever leave you? Who would make corn fritters for my special girl?"

Gina grinned. She liked talking with her grandmother. Grandma always had plenty of time to listen. She was never in a terrible hurry like her mother usually was. Gina leaned on her elbow and whispered, "What's the matter with Dwayne? Why is he so mean? How come he thinks he can bust into my room and tell me to turn off my radio? This is *my* house."

"It's Dwayne's house too."

Gina dropped back on her pillow with a groan.

"Anyway, he's not mean," continued Grandma. "He just

28

likes to read a lot, and your radio is a bit loud at times. Maybe you could try turning it down."

"I never used to have to turn it down. Everything used to be perfect," said Gina. "Dwayne's a grouch."

"It's been hard for Dwayne, his parents' divorce, moving away from Lakeville, and everything. Try to be more patient with him."

Gina turned aside as the tears rushed to her eyes. "He never says anything nice to me. He hates me."

Grandma sighed. "I'll let you in on a little secret. I was running the sweeper in Dwayne's room the other day, and I found a picture that Dwayne had made. It was a picture of his mother. His other mother. Do you understand?"

Gina nodded. "He misses his mother, doesn't he?"

"Exactly. She moved so far away, you know."

Gina wasn't sure what it would be like to have her parents divorce. She couldn't remember her own father. He had died when she was seven months old. She kissed Grandma good night and watched her leave.

Gradually, Gina forgot about Dwayne as Carrie's words drifted back to her: "I refuse to sleep in a haunted cabin." She pulled her sheet to her chin. Just because it was a spooky place didn't mean a ghost lived there. Grandma didn't believe a silly ghost story, and neither did she. It was only an old house. A family named Owens had lived there at one time. Five children had filled the rooms with noise. Sophie Owens's mother had tended a garden beside the cabin. There really wasn't anything to be afraid of. She fell asleep clutching the beaded Indian necklace that hung around her neck.

The next morning, Gina officially opened Camp Kickapoo. Carrie, Tiffany, and she watched as Richard and Jed set up a faded green tent down near the woods. The boys were coming to Camp Kickapoo whether the girls liked it or not.

"There's definitely something wrong with our tent," said Jed. He pushed his glasses back on his nose and studied it. The tent leaned oddly to the left. "According to my calculations, the tent shouldn't be looking like this."

"What's wrong?" said Richard. "It looks good to me. It's just missing a pole, that's all. I'll get that old mop handle from the shed."

"All right, everybody line up right here," ordered Gina. She tapped the ground with her camp director's stick. "I want to welcome you all to Camp Kickapoo."

The campers pushed and shoved themselves into a straight line. Carrie held a can of pop in one hand and took a few gulps now and then. Tiffany tried to stand next to Carrie, but with Ozzie the snake draped over Tiffany's shoulders, Carrie kept inching away.

"I'm sure most of you remember what a fun time we had last year at Camp Kickapoo—"

"I almost drowned when our canoe sank," said Carrie.

"I almost choked to death on grasshopper stew," said Jed.

"I was almost eaten alive when that monster grizzly bear chased me at speeds that reached one hundred miles an hour," said Richard.

"That was a 'possum," said Jed.

"It was a grizzly." Richard held up a fist to Jed's chin.

30

"There're bears in these woods?" asked Tiffany.

"Please, please," said Gina. "There are no bears in these woods. Richard just can't see too well."

"He can't hear too well, either," said Carrie, "because of all the beans in his ears."

"I don't have beans in my ears," said Richard, shifting his fist from Jed's chin to Carrie's chin.

"Pass in your money and your permission slips." Gina walked up and down the line as she took two dollars and permission slips from all the campers and put them in her pocket. "Very good. I see that all your parents have signed your slips and everyone brought their money."

"We'd better get something better than grasshopper stew for our two dollars," said Richard. "You ought to pay *us* to eat that stuff. A dollar a grasshopper."

"Be quiet, Richard." Gina walked back and forth in front of the campers. "As Kickapoo campers, we are all for one, and one for all. Let's hear it!"

"All for one, and one for all!" everyone shouted.

"We help fellow campers at all times," said Gina.

"We help fellow campers at all times!"

"Through rain and sleet and snow and floods," continued Gina.

"This is summer," said Richard. "It doesn't snow in summer."

"We might get a little rain, but by my calculations, there hasn't been a flood around here since the flood of '37," said Jed.

"Forget it!" Gina smacked her stick in her hand and glared at Richard and Jed. It was not going to be easy hav-

31

ing Richard the Nerd and Jed the Math Professor at Camp Kickapoo.

She cleared her throat. "We will now sing our camp song. It goes like this." With great gusto, Gina sang out the words of the song she had made up that morning to the tune of "O Tannenbaum":

> Oh Kickapoo, Camp Kickapoo,
> We love your good grasshopper stew.
> Oh Kickapoo, dear Kickapoo,
> To you we'll be forever true.
> We'll roast our hot dogs on a fire
> And sing our camp songs like a choir.
> Oh Kickapoo, Camp Kickapoo,
> The best camp on Clark Avenue.

She stopped and waited for applause. There was only an eerie silence. "Are you finished yet?" Richard finally asked with a look of genuine pain on his face.

"I like last year's song a whole lot better," said Jed.

"Well," said Gina, disappointed in their lack of enthusiasm for all her hard work, "this is this year's song, and everybody has to learn it." She led the campers in a rousing round of singing and was pleased with the results. She couldn't help but notice how Tiffany's birdlike voice rang out above all the others. Her new sister was quite a good singer.

When the song ended, Gina continued, "As some of you know, Camp Kickapoo is named in honor of the Indians who used to roam these woods. The Kickapoos hunted buf-

falo right here on this very spot." She hit the ground with her stick.

"Kickapoo, Kickapoo," sang Tiffany. She swung her blue canvas bag back and forth.

"Kickapoo, spit in your shoe—" began Richard.

"Attention!" shouted Gina. She walked up and down the line, shaking her stick at each camper as she went. "At Camp Kickapoo, we will do everything like they did it two hundred years ago. We will take good care of the land, just like the Indians did. We'll eat over an open fire. We won't throw cans in the creek or anything. Only pigs do that. And we won't break any twigs when we walk through the woods. This is a back-to-nature camp. You can't have any new stuff, anything invented after say, 1800. Get it?"

"I get it," said Richard. He reached for a box of crackers that stood on the picnic table. "Is it time to eat yet? I'm hungry."

"Oh no you don't," said Gina. She confiscated the box of crackers. "We're supposed to be settlers out here in the great big wilderness. Brave pioneers fighting off wild animals. Trailblazers cutting a path through the deep forest. We can't eat Town House crackers. They didn't have them back then."

"Come on," said Richard. "We almost starved to death last year. I hate grasshopper stew."

"I refuse to eat grasshopper stew," said Carrie.

"What does it taste like?" asked Tiffany.

"It's worse than worms," said Jed.

"It's even worse than spinach," said Richard.

"Yuck!" Tiffany made a terrible face.

"Gee, maybe we'll get lucky and have something good this year, like spider soup," said Jed, "with some crunchy beetles thrown in."

"I'm in charge of food, and nobody will starve to death," said Gina. "This has to go." She took the can of pop from Carrie's hand and placed it on the lid of Ozzie's aquarium, which had been brought down to the patio.

"What am I supposed to drink?" asked Carrie.

"Good fresh water," said Gina.

"Water? Are you kidding?"

"Pioneers drink water," stated Gina.

Carrie pointed to the snake that hung around Tiffany's neck. "You've got to get rid of that beast."

"No!" shouted Tiffany. "Snakes were invented before 1800. Ozzie isn't hurting anything." She stroked her snake.

"He'll have to go back in his aquarium when we go to the cabin," said Gina. "I sure wouldn't want a snake loose in the cabin." She glanced back at Jed, who was busy taking pictures of Ozzie with his new camera. "No cameras allowed at Camp Kickapoo, Jed. Hand it over."

"But I'm the camp photographer," protested Jed.

"Not anymore." Gina reached for Jed's camera.

She hung the camera strap around her neck and noticed Richard focusing his new binoculars. "What are you staring at?"

"Your nose. I never knew what a mammoth schnozzola you've got. Geezo! Sort of like a watermelon growing out of a pinhead."

Gina snatched Richard's binoculars and hung them over her neck on top of the camera. "These have to go. Pioneers didn't have binoculars. They used their eyes. What kind of pioneers are you anyway?"

"Aw, come on. I can't do any birdwatching if I don't have my binoculars," complained Richard.

"Too bad," said Gina. "Uh oh. This has to go." She pointed with her stick to Carrie's new watch. "Pioneers did not wear watches. Not ones like this anyway."

"Wait a minute. This is my brand-new watch. It glows in the dark."

"Awesome," said Jed. "Let's see."

"Hand it over," ordered Gina.

"Oh, nuts!" Carrie unfastened her watch and dropped it into Gina's extended hand. "How will I know when cartoons are on?"

"Pioneers didn't watch cartoons. They didn't have TVs."

"Gee, are you sure this is going to be fun, being a pioneer?" asked Richard.

"Of course it's going to be fun," said Gina. "Now listen. It's time to fix up our beds. You boys take your stuff to the tent, and we'll take our things to the cabin." Gina motioned for Carrie and Tiffany to follow her.

The girls picked up their sleeping bags and suitcases and marched down the path to the cabin. The boys threw their camping equipment into the tent after getting an old mop handle from the shed to substitute for the missing tent pole.

A few minutes later, they all met around the sundial that stood in front of Gina's grandmother's rose garden. "Instead of using watches," explained Gina, "we are going to tell time with our sundial." She was about to explain how the sundial worked when she was interrupted by Tiffany.

"I have to go to the bathroom. Wait for me, okay?" Tiffany turned to leave.

"Just a minute. You can't use a real bathroom. Pioneers didn't have indoor plumbing."

Tiffany's mouth dropped in amazement. "Well, what am I supposed to do?"

Gina thought a moment. "We'll have to build a latrine in the woods. This is a back-to-nature camp, remember? Come on." She found a shovel in the shed and led the campers a few feet into the woods, where she began to dig a hole.

"What do you think you're doing?" asked Carrie.

"I'm digging a hole to use for our bathroom. That's what the pioneers did," said Gina. "Here, help me." She held out the shovel to Carrie.

"I'm not digging a dumb hole," said Carrie as she folded her arms across her chest.

Tiffany began to hop from one foot to the other. Ozzie's head bobbed gently up and down. "I've got to go. Now!"

"Any camper who doesn't help dig the latrine doesn't get to be in Camp Kickapoo," stated Gina. Carrie reached for the shovel and began to dig.

Richard held his chin high and spoke slowly. "I'm going to be Daniel Boone, the great trailblazer. Daniel Boone didn't dig latrines."

"Well, maybe Daniel Boone didn't, but you are," said Carrie. "It's your turn." She handed Richard the shovel.

"But this is hard," complained Richard as he pushed the shovel deep into the ground. The talking ceased when the children heard the sound of metal striking metal.

"What'd you hit?" asked Jed.

Richard lifted a shovelful of dirt and exposed a portion of a metal box. "A coffin!"

Everyone dropped to the ground and began clawing at the dirt around the box. "Move over," cried Tiffany. "Let me see."

After more digging, the tin box, about the size of a large shoe box, was pulled from the ground. Richard brushed the dirt from the top and tried to lift the lid, but the box was sealed tight.

"That's no coffin," said Jed.

"Buried treasure," said Carrie. "Wow! We've struck it rich!"

"Hurry up," said Tiffany. "What's inside?"

"Who's got a screwdriver?" yelled Richard. He clawed at the lid.

"Here," said Gina. "Use this stick. Pioneers didn't have screwdrivers."

Richard tried to pry the lid open with the stick, but it was no use.

"Let's heat it," said Jed. "Heat'll make it get bigger, and the lid will come off. I learned that in science class."

"Yeah, and whatever is inside will be cooked," said Gina. "What if there's a dinosaur egg in here?"

"Then we'll have cooked dinosaur egg for lunch," said Jed. "Better than grasshopper stew."

After pulling on the lid one more time, Gina gave up

38

and ran to the garage. She returned in a minute with a screwdriver, which she twisted underneath the lid. The lid suddenly came off, revealing a wadded piece of blue cloth. Gina reached for the blue bundle and felt something hard inside.

"Something's in here," she said.

"Let me see!" cried Tiffany. Tiffany moved in closer, and Carrie screamed as Ozzie the snake began to wrap around her neck.

"Get that snake out of here!" screeched Carrie. But no one paid any attention to her. They all leaned over Gina and watched as she unwrapped what was in the blue cloth.

4

A VANISHING ACT

A doll tumbled out and dropped into her lap. "Oh, wow, some treasure," said Jed. "A dumb doll. Whoopie. I thought we'd found something really good like gold doubloons or a pirate's dagger."

"I'd rather find a dinosaur egg," said Richard.

Despite their disappointment, Richard and Jed crowded closer along with the others as they examined the strange find.

The doll was unlike any they had ever seen, with a satiny green dress and high-topped leather shoes. Thick red curls fell loosely around the delicate porcelain face. The eyelids opened, revealing brown eyes that stared up at them.

"I want it!" cried Tiffany. Her dirty hands reached for the doll.

"Don't touch," said Gina, quickly lifting the doll out of her sister's reach. Tiffany dropped her hands and frowned.

"Who buried this doll, anyway?" asked Carrie.

"Do you think we could get any money for it?" asked Jed.

"I wonder how long it's been buried," said Gina. "It looks ancient." The doll resembled a girl of about nine or ten years old.

"My gosh, do you know what we've done?" said Richard. "This is probably a doll cemetery, and we've dug up a dead doll."

"Don't be ridiculous," said Gina. She rocked the doll in her arms and smoothed the wrinkled dress. "You poor doll, you poor, poor doll," she crooned softly as she gazed down at the doll's sad face.

"Let me hold her," cried Tiffany. "Please, Gina!" But Gina ignored her sister as she turned to the other campers. The older four discussed what to do with the doll as they walked out of the woods and up the sloping lawn to the patio. Tiffany came along a few steps behind the rest. Ozzie swung gently from her left arm as she walked.

Gina and Carrie decided to go to Carrie's house and get a doll book. Carrie's mother collected antiques of all sorts and had several books about dolls.

"Let me hold the doll, please?" said Tiffany. She ran to the aquarium, lifted the lid, and carefully dropped her snake inside. She reached for the doll.

"Okay, okay. Sit right here and don't move," said Gina as she patted the picnic table bench. She carefully placed the small doll in Tiffany's arms. Delighted, Tiffany took the doll and began to rock it back and forth, softly humming. She never looked up as Gina said, "We'll be back before you can finish singing a lullaby." Gina waved to Richard and Jed, who were already running down the ravine to the creek that ran along one side of the yard.

41

It was forty-five minutes before the girls returned. They had spent more time at Carrie's house than they had anticipated, trapped by Carrie's mother, who had insisted on hearing all about the doll. Mrs. Carlton had pulled a large book titled *Collecting Antique Dolls for Fun and Profit* from a bookshelf, and the three of them had studied page after page.

"I have to leave for a meeting now," Mrs. Carlton had told them, "but as soon as I get home, I want to see that doll." She had pointed excitedly to a picture of a porcelain doll made during the 1930s. "From how you describe it, the doll sounds like this one. Three hundred dollars!" Gina had never seen Carrie's mother so excited, except on the day when she had taken them to an estate auction and had bought a nineteenth-century wooden doll for fifteen dollars.

The girls had run all the way down Clark Avenue to Gina's backyard. It was deserted. Gina slapped the picnic table. "I told Tiffany to stay right here. We weren't gone that long, were we?"

"They're down by the creek," said Carrie. "I hear them." The girls ran to the side of the ravine and looked over the edge. Jed and Richard skipped pebbles across the water in the creek below.

"Hey, Richard, where's Tiffany?" hollered Gina. The boys looked up and shrugged their shoulders.

"She's probably in the house," said Carrie. "Let's look."

"What if she's not? Then Mom'll know I've lost her. We'd better check the cabin first. I bet that's where she went."

They ran to the cabin. "Tiffany!" called Gina as she opened the door and walked inside. "Are you in here?" Her voice bounced around the empty rooms.

"Hey, look at this," said Carrie. She pointed to three wet spots on the floor near the stairway. "Looks like . . . blood."

Gina dropped to her knees and examined the mysterious red spots. "Still wet." She reached toward the spots but suddenly drew her hand back.

"Let's go!" Carrie pulled Gina's arm.

"Tiffany!" called Gina, more urgently than before. She dashed up the stairs two at a time and turned into the bedroom on the right. Nothing.

Gina ran back to the other bedroom and skidded to an abrupt halt when she saw Tiffany. Her sister was curled up in her sleeping bag with her stuffed tiger under her arm.

"She's in here," Gina called. Carrie climbed the steps and entered the room as Tiffany opened her eyes.

"We've been searching all over for you," said Gina.

Tiffany looked around the room, trying to remember where she was. "I had to go to the bathroom." And then she grinned. "I used the latrine."

"Oh." Gina glanced around the room. "Where'd you put the doll?"

Tiffany pointed to her sleeping bag. "It was here."

"What do you mean? Where is it now?"

Tiffany yawned. "I thought I heard someone up here. I came up to see who it was, but there wasn't anybody. So I thought I'd take a nap. I got tired of waiting." She yawned again, covering her mouth with her hand.

"You heard someone?" said Gina and Carrie together. "Upstairs here?"

"Well, I thought I did," answered Tiffany, "but I guess I didn't." She patted her pillow. "I put the doll right here." She looked confused. "Where is it?"

"That's a good question," said Carrie.

"It probably fell inside the sleeping bag," said Gina. She reached inside the bag and screamed as her hand touched the cold head of a snake. Ozzie's tongue flicked at her fingers.

Gina tore back the top of the bag. "Tiffany! Get your snake out of this cabin. Do you hear me? No snakes at Camp Kickapoo."

"Ozzie's not hurting anything. He likes it here."

"No snakes allowed. Right, Carrie?" said Gina.

"Right!"

"Come on. Let's go." Gina pulled Tiffany to her feet. "Boy, we can't leave for five minutes without something happening. I bet Richard and Jed were messing around up here. They probably hid in the closet or maybe out on the roof."

Gina inspected all four upstairs windows, two at the back of the cabin and two at the front. The front windows opened to the porch roof. An oak tree spread its branches across one corner of the roof.

Before leaving, Gina and Carrie overturned every sleeping bag and looked into every suitcase in hopes of finding the sad-faced doll, but it had vanished.

"Do you think Richard and Jed got the doll?" asked Carrie.

"Of course. Who else?"

"I want my doll," said Tiffany.

"Your doll?" said Gina.

"Richard dug it up," said Carrie.

"It's my doll," stated Tiffany. "You gave her to me."

"I only gave her to you to hold," explained Gina. "For five minutes." They argued about the doll all the way back to the yard.

Jed and Richard were studying the sundial. "Hey, isn't it lunchtime yet?" called Richard. "I'm starved."

"Do you guys have the doll?" asked Gina.

Jed laughed. "Oh, yeah. We just couldn't wait to play with it."

"Tiffany had it," said Richard.

Gina shook her head. "She did. But it's gone now. This is not one bit funny."

"That doll's worth three hundred dollars, Mom said," added Carrie.

Richard whistled. "That's a lot."

"You mean you really didn't take it?" asked Gina.

"Of course we didn't take it," said Richard.

The campers grew quiet as Gina's grandmother walked across the yard toward them. She wore gardening gloves and carried a shovel in her right hand. "What's all this ruckus about?" she asked.

Gina decided to tell her grandmother about the mysterious doll—about how they had dug a latrine and uncovered a tin box with a porcelain-head doll inside. She showed her grandmother the box. Her grandmother gently touched it as though touching fragile glass and then shook her head.

45

"Sophie's treasure box. My, my, my," she said, more to herself than to them. And then a bit louder, "Where did you say you found this?"

"Over here." The campers led Gina's grandmother to the hole in the ground where the box had been found.

"So this is where she hid it." Grandma stared down at the hole.

"Who?" said Gina.

"My friend. Sophie. Sophie Owens. That girl I told you about who used to live here."

"You mean we found Sophie's old doll?" asked Gina. "Why'd she bury it?"

"It's *my* doll," said Grandma. "But Sophie always wanted to play with it. She never had a real store-bought doll of her own. I gave it to her one day, and then I went with my family to visit my cousins for a few weeks over in Piketown. Sophie left for Oklahoma before we ever got back. I never even said good-bye to her. She left me a letter saying she had buried my doll in her treasure box for safekeeping until I got back from Piketown."

"Why did she do that?" asked Gina.

"That was just the way Sophie was. She liked to play games. She was especially fond of treasure hunts. In her letter she said she was going to send me a special map from Oklahoma to show me where she'd buried the treasure box."

"Did she?" the campers asked when Grandma paused.

Gina saw a tear in the corner of her eye. "Sophie never had a chance to write me a second letter. She died on the way to Oklahoma. Meningitis, I believe it was."

46

"Oh, Grandma." Gina put her arms around her grandmother.

"After a while, I went out and searched for my doll. It was like my final good-bye to Sophie, since she'd been the last one to hold it. I must have dug twenty-five holes all around the woods, anywhere I thought Sophie might have buried her treasure box, but I never could find it."

Grandma gingerly lifted the lid of the box and was startled to find it empty. Gina bit her lower lip when she saw her grandmother's look of disappointment.

"Where is it?" asked Grandma.

"Well, Grandma, the doll has . . ." Gina gulped and looked at Tiffany. "Tiffany had it and she . . . she lost it."

"I did not!" cried Tiffany.

Grandma's face fell. Her disappointment was more than Gina could bear. "Don't worry, Grandma. We're going to find it for you. It's just been misplaced." Gina patted her grandmother's arm and tried to explain how she and Carrie had left for a few minutes and returned to find the doll missing.

"I did not lose it!" repeated Tiffany. She kicked Gina's leg.

"Ouch! You little—"

"Girls!" Grandma put one arm around Gina's shoulder and one around Tiffany's. "I guess that doll doesn't ever want me to find her, does she?" She walked slowly back to her garden and bent over her rosebushes. Gina heard her murmur something about "After all these years," as she walked away.

"Oh, Tiffany, look what you did," said Gina.

Tiffany's chin began to quiver, and she turned around and ran back to the house. She sat down next to Ozzie's aquarium and shouted, "I didn't lose it. Don't ever say that."

"I'm starved," said Richard. "When do we eat?"

"Richard! How can you think of food at a time like this?" said Gina. "We've got to find Grandma's doll."

"Not on an empty stomach. I'm hungry."

Gina's stomach was growling too. Being a camp director was not easy. Should they eat first or search for the missing doll? Gina decided to keep her hungry campers happy with a quick lunch. "Okay, we'll bake our bread first and then go on a food hunt."

"Good!" said Richard.

"That shouldn't take too long. Maybe we'll find the doll in the woods while we're hunting for food." Gina looked imploringly toward Richard. "Are you absolutely positive you didn't take it?"

"I'm positive," said Richard. "Now how about going to McDonald's?"

Gina shook her head. "We are pioneers, Richard. Pioneers do not go to McDonald's."

After picking up a few supplies from her house, Gina directed the campers down a path in the ravine, across the creek on a bridge made of rocks, and up to a grassy field. "Now, campers, to bake bread pioneer style, we have to gather the wheat, grind it up in a bowl, add some yeast and sugar and milk, and bake it in a hot oven."

"Get serious," said Jed.

"If you don't work, you don't eat," said Gina. "That's what Captain John Smith told the people at Jamestown."

"This isn't Jamestown, and you're not John Smith," said Jed.

"Maybe so, but you still have to work." Gina pulled some tall plants and shook the seeds into an old wooden salad bowl. With a rock she ground the seeds into a coarse meal.

"Are you sure this is wheat?" asked Richard. He took a bowl from Gina's bag and dropped seeds into it.

"Well, if it's not, it looks just like it, and I've already eaten it, so it won't kill you." Gina left her campers busily grinding seeds while she went back to her house. As she crossed the patio, she spotted Ozzie in his aquarium. Tiffany was gone. She entered the kitchen and came back out with an envelope of yeast, a cup of sugar, a carton of milk, and a small bag of flour.

The campers sat in the field and pounded and stirred the ground-up plants, sugar, yeast, milk, and flour until blobs of gray stuck to each bowl. "Looks good," said Gina. "I think it's time to knead your bread now."

"I don't need this at all," said Richard.

"Knead, Richard, knead. Like this." Gina scooped up her blob of dough and squeezed it between her palms. She folded it and squeezed again.

"How do we cook this guck?" asked Richard, after he finished kneading his dough.

"In the oven. Follow me." Gina led everyone back across the creek, up the path to her yard, to the boulder that stood near the shed. Right here on this rock." She dropped her bread dough onto the rock. "This rock is hot. Feel it. Put your bread here and we'll hunt for some berries and nuts. By the time we get back, the sun will have baked it. We'll have good homemade bread, warm from the oven."

"But I'm hungry now," complained Richard.

"I suppose we have to squash the berries and nuts to make peanut butter and jelly?" said Jed.

Gina raised her eyebrows. "Hey, what a good idea!"

Carrie had not said much as she struggled to make her small loaf of bread. She placed it on the rock and finally revealed what she had been thinking. "Gina, I've got this funny feeling we are being watched again. Just like when we were in the cabin." The chattering grew quiet. "I think that story about the ghost is true. There *is* a ghost."

"Oh, Carrie, stop it," said Gina.

"Listen to me. I think Sophie Owens has come back home. I mean, the ghost of Sophie Owens." Carrie paused. "That was *her* we heard in the cabin yesterday. She wanted us out of her house. Remember?"

"Don't be silly, Carrie. That was Jed, wasn't it, Jed?"

Jed looked confused. "What?"

"That was you in the cabin yesterday, right?" said Gina. "The one who yelled 'Get out of my house!' "

"I wasn't in the cabin yesterday," said Jed. Gina eyed him suspiciously, trying to figure out if he was telling the truth.

"Were you?" Gina asked Richard.

"Don't look at me."

"And today Tiffany said she heard someone upstairs," continued Carrie. "Richard and Jed were down at the creek. I'm telling you that the ghost of Sophie Owens has come back to her home, and she's found the old doll. The one she always wanted to play with. She must have taken it right out of Tiffany's arms while she was asleep!" Carrie talked fast as she put the pieces of the puzzle together and realized just what it meant.

"A ghost?" said Jed.

"The ghost of Sophie Owens?" said Richard.

"That's the most ridiculous thing I ever heard in my whole life," said Gina. "I don't believe in ghosts."

"Well, I do," said Carrie. "And now I know who's been watching us from the woods." She shivered as she looked toward the trees.

THE SECRET SUITCASE

"Wow!" said Richard. "A real ghost in our very own woods."

"Let's have a ghost hunt," said Jed, always eager for adventure.

"I'm going home. I'm packing my stuff, and I'm going home right now," said Carrie. "I'm scared."

Gina sat for a few minutes lost in thought. "I want that doll," she finally said. "It belongs to my grandmother, and I'm going to find it for her. Thursday is Grandma's birthday. Wouldn't that make the best birthday present ever? To find her lost doll?" She twisted the beads of her necklace.

"Forget it," said Carrie. "I'm not getting near the cabin ever again. Never."

Gina studied the woods. Sun rays filtered down through the branches. Birds called to one another, and a woodpecker could be heard pecking into a nearby tree trunk. "Didn't you see how disappointed my grandmother was? That doll means a lot to her. I'd give anything to find it for her."

"Good. You find it. I'm going home," said Carrie. She

started to leave and then remembered that her suitcase and sleeping bag were in the cabin.

"Bring my sleeping bag and stuff over to my house, will you? Please?" Carrie looked from Gina to Richard to Jed.

"You don't have to leave, Carrie," said Gina. "We're not going on a ghost hunt, because there isn't any ghost. But we are going on a doll hunt, because I know exactly where that doll is. And it wasn't a ghost that took it." There was an unmistakable ring of confidence in Gina's voice.

"Who did?" asked Carrie.

"Tiffany."

"Tiffany?" Carrie, Richard, and Jed exchanged glances of disbelief.

"Of course Tiffany," said Gina. "Who else? Tiffany loves dolls. She always wants to play with mine. You heard her, Carrie. She was begging me for that doll. She thinks it's hers. The way I see it, she went in the house, hid the doll in her suitcase where she hides everything, and then went back to the cabin and pretended to be asleep. Some actress, huh?"

"I don't think so," said Carrie. "Tiffany wasn't acting."

"She thinks all my stuff belongs to her. I'm sure she took it," said Gina.

"Let's go find out," said Jed.

"Good! Follow me." Gina led the way through the yard and into her house. Gina's parents were both at work. Dwayne stood by the open refrigerator door, studying the contents. He held a plate of cold pizza in his left hand. Tiffany was playing with a game of Cootie on the dining room table and singing at the top of her voice. She stopped singing when she saw them. Grandma, half dozing, was watching TV. Without a word, the campers marched quickly from one room to the next and finally climbed the stairway.

They piled into Gina's room and closed the door behind them. "I don't see the doll," said Richard.

"Shhh! Keep your voice down," warned Gina. "She might follow us up here. It's over this way." She knelt down beside Tiffany's bed and quickly dragged the suitcase out from under it. "This is where she hides things. Oh no, I forgot."

"What's the matter?" asked Carrie.

"The key. It's in the bottom of the aquarium." Gina looked over her shoulder, but the aquarium was not there.

"The aquarium's on the patio," said Jed.

"Okay, let's go." Gina led the way back down the steps, through the living room, past Grandma and Dwayne and Tiffany.

When the campers reached the aquarium, Gina asked Richard to get the key from the pebbles at the bottom. Richard eyed the snake coiled in the warm sun, sleeping.

"Why me?" he asked.

"Because . . . because Ozzie doesn't like me," said Gina. "He likes you. Hurry up. The key is right there." She pointed to the left corner of the aquarium and jumped back when Ozzie opened his eyes and lifted his head.

"You're just scared." Richard laughed. "Ha ha! Scared of a little old snake." He reached into the aquarium. The snake moved. Carrie screamed. Richard jerked his hand out fast.

"Oh, Richard! You almost had it." Gina looked nervously behind her toward the back door.

"Does this snake bite?" asked Richard.

"Of course not," said Gina. "Get the key."

Richard stuck his hand back in the aquarium and wiggled his fingers into the pebbles. "Can't find it."

Gina bit her lip. "Look for it. It's there."

Richard shook his head. Ozzie slithered slowly away from Richard's hand. "Not here," said Richard.

Gina plunged her hand into the aquarium. "It's got to be here." Her fingers felt around in the pebbles. She quickly found the key, pulled it out, and waved it in the air with a whoop of joy.

"Shhh!" cautioned Carrie.

They wound their way back through the house, up the stairs, and into the bedroom. Gina unlocked the suitcase and lifted the lid. Surprise and disappointment swept through her as she surveyed the contents. The missing doll was not there.

Gina held her nose and pointed to a half-eaten cheese sandwich. "So this is what I've been smelling. And grapes. I might have known she keeps her grapes stashed away up here."

"Who's this?" asked Carrie as she picked up a photo of a little girl.

"Hmmm. That must be Tiffany's friend from Lakeville," said Gina. "Sarah. She talks about her all the time. One time she pretended to call her long distance. She pretended Sarah was on the other end, and she talked for an hour."

The campers rummaged through some papers, two plastic dinosaurs, a box with a pink pearl necklace, some wrapped bubble gum, and a few other prize possessions of Tiffany's. Leaving the suitcase open, they searched the rest of the room, including the closet and all of the dresser drawers.

"Where'd you get this?" asked Carrie. She pointed to a framed picture drawn with pastels that sat on Gina's bed table.

Gina's face grew red with embarrassment. "It's just a stupid picture Kevin drew in art class."

"Is that supposed to be you?" asked Carrie.

"Yeah. It's stupid, isn't it? Kevin draws pictures of everybody."

"Kevin loves Gina. Kevin loves Gina," sang Richard and Jed together. They poked Gina playfully.

"He does not!"

Gina was about to say something else when the bedroom door opened. The talking ceased as Tiffany took one step into the room. "What are you doing in my suitcase?" She ran over to Gina, slammed her suitcase lid, and pushed it back under the bed. "This is *my* suitcase!"

"We were just looking for the doll," said Gina. She instantly felt regret for her words when she saw Tiffany's hurt expression. Her stepsister had never looked at her that way before.

"I told you I lost the doll. I don't know where it is." Tiffany's eyes filled with tears as she said, "You promised me, Gina. You said you would never open my suitcase."

"I'm sorry, Tiffany. I'll never open it again." Gina held up her right hand and smiled. "Kickapoo's honor."

"Kickapoo, spit in your shoe!" cried Tiffany as she ran from the room.

Gina slowly lowered her hand. Some honor, she thought. She had promised never to open Tiffany's suitcase, and she had broken her promise. A good pioneer would not break a promise. She put the suitcase key on Tiffany's pillow.

"Don't you want your beautiful picture that Kevin drew?" crooned Richard. He picked up the picture from the nightstand and began to kiss it, making sloppy, smacking noises.

Gina grabbed the picture from Richard's hands, tossed it on her bed, and pulled Richard out the door. Carrie and Jed followed behind. "I don't ever want to hear Kevin's name," she said.

"Me neither," said Jed. "I want lunch. I'm hungry."

"We're going on a food hunt right now," said Gina. If her campers didn't get something to eat soon, they might all leave. "We'll hunt for nuts and berries down by the creek. And then after lunch, we'll start an official search for the doll."

"Do you still think Tiffany took it and hid it somewhere?" asked Carrie.

"I don't know," said Gina.

They hiked down the steep path from the edge of Gina's yard to the creek bottom where the blackberries grew. As they searched the bushes for berries, Clyde the cat darted between them, pouncing on leaves as they fluttered across the path.

"I hate to tell you this," said a voice behind them, "but this is not blackberry season. They're not ripe yet."

Everyone spun around, only to see Kevin step out from behind a tree.

"Gosh, Kevin, you scared us to death," said Gina. Her face flushed pink.

"Here comes Gina's boyfriend," sang Richard. Gina clapped her hand over his mouth.

"I just thought I'd save you a little time," said Kevin. "I have a whole quart of strawberries in my refrigerator. Do you want any?"

"How did you know we were hunting for berries?" asked Gina.

"I heard you talking."

"This is Camp Kickapoo," said Jed. "We have to hunt for our food. We can't get food out of a refrigerator. That's too modern."

"Our great leader," said Richard as he pried Gina's hand from his mouth, "only lets us eat nuts, berries, snails, grasshopper stew, homemade bread, and stuff like that. No strawberries from the grocery store."

"Well, I hope you find some grub," said Kevin. "We've got chicken in our refrigerator. Sure you don't want any?"

"No, thanks," said Gina. "We'll just keep hunting for food out here in the wilderness."

"Okay," said Kevin. He sounded disappointed. "Good luck." He turned and disappeared into the woods.

Gina led the campers farther along the edge of the creek. "Something's got to be ripe. How did the pioneers ever find anything to eat?"

"They must have gathered their food all summer and stored it in refrigerators in the wintertime," said Richard.

"Pioneers didn't have refrigerators," said Gina.

"I know what they did," said Carrie. "They dug out holes in the ground, deep down where it was cold, and kept their food there."

"Hey, we could do that," said Gina.

"I already dug a latrine, and I'm not digging any more holes," said Richard.

"Why not? Then we could have our own fresh water and lower all our food down where it's cool," said Gina.

"What's wrong with getting our water from the faucet at the back of the house?" asked Richard.

"You always want to do everything the easy way," said Gina. "That's no fun."

They had reached the oak tree that shadowed the creek with its massive branches. Richard threw down his paper bag and jumped up to grab the vine that swayed in the breeze. "Last one across the creek is a monkey's uncle," he shouted as he ran a few steps backward and then swung out over the creek with a loud Tarzan yodel. He landed with a thud in the mud on the other side.

Jed, Carrie, and Gina took their turns sailing through the air, clutching the gnarled vine, skimming across the top of the water, and landing on the muddy bank. They crossed the creek again on the rock bridge and continued the search for blackberries and nuts. Gina glanced up once and noticed Kevin swinging on the vine across the creek.

"I know where we can find some nuts," called Richard. "Back at my house. Come on." He waved the campers to follow him, and they all raced one another to the Carltons' house.

Gina protested all the way but gave up when she saw the jar of salted peanuts and a cardboard container of raspberries. Her stomach had been growling for an hour. "I doubt if pioneers ate peanuts from a jar, but just this once, we'll make an exception. Tonight, though, we hunt for snails. I know we can find snails."

"Snails?" asked Carrie. "Are you trying to kill us?"

After lunch, the campers walked back down Clark Avenue and into Gina's backyard. Richard and Jed went off by themselves while Gina and Carrie went to the rock and tested their loaves of bread. "Too bad. Still too soft. These are going to be good when they're done. If it were only a warmer day, they would have baked by now," said Gina.

"Sure," said Carrie. "We'll eat them tonight with our snails. Snail sandwiches. I can't wait."

The girls turned around just in time to see Richard totter across the yard on a pair of stilts. An Indian chief headdress was tied around his waist with the feathers shooting out behind him.

"Save me!" cried Carrie. "The long-legged beanbrained sapsucker is loose again. Help!"

"I'm no sapsucker. I'm an ostrich," said Richard. "Do you like my costume?" Before Carrie could answer, Richard lost his balance and fell on the tent, collapsing the poles and bringing the tent to the ground. Clyde, who had been sleeping inside, shot out from under the rubble with an earsplitting yowl.

"Look what you made me do," he said.

"Way to go!" said Gina. The girls watched as Jed pulled Richard loose from the tangle of canvas, stilts, and poles.

"Thanks," said Richard as he brushed himself off. He and Jed pulled the tent poles back into position.

"I'm ready to give my bird talk now. Okay, Gina?" Richard pulled a piece of paper from his back pocket and cleared his throat. Ever since he had gotten his new binoculars and a book about birds, he had become Clark Avenue's bird expert. He climbed onto his stilts and stuck out his tail feathers.

"Some other time," said Gina. "I really want to have our official search for the doll before it gets dark. Come on, it's got to be around here somewhere."

Richard strutted around in a circle on his stilts, ignoring Gina. "My talk today is on the African ostrich."

"How nice. My brother the ostrich," said Carrie as she nudged Gina with her elbow. Gina gave up. She plopped down on the grass to watch Richard's show. Clyde hopped into her lap.

"The ostrich is the biggest bird alive, about three hundred pounds. Almost as big as Carrie." Richard jumped off the stilts, puffed his cheeks full of air, and crossed his eyes. "The male ostrich," he continued, "is much handsomer than the female."

"Boys are always better looking than girls," said Jed with a laugh. Carrie and Gina stuck their fingers in their ears and closed their eyes.

"The male ostrich," continued Richard, "has beautiful black and white feathers, long legs, a long neck, and a real tiny head about the size of a tennis ball."

"Sounds like you, Richard," said Gina as she pulled her fingers from her ears. "Tennis ball brain."

Richard sprang at the girls, hissing like a snake. Carrie screamed. "That's how ostriches sound. Weird, huh?"

"They do not," said Gina.

"Yes, they do. I heard one at the zoo." Richard took off running around the yard, flapping his arms up and down. "Ostriches can't fly, but they can run like you wouldn't believe, almost as fast as a car."

Jed jumped up and loped along behind Richard. "Sit down, Jed," ordered Gina. "This is Camp Kickapoo, not the Cincinnati Zoo."

"And did you ever hear how an ostrich gets scared and buries its head in the ground?" Richard stopped running, and Jed slammed into his tail feathers. "Well, it isn't true. Nobody can bury his head in the ground. I know. I tried it. I could barely breathe."

Gina stood up. "That's enough, Richard. Thank you very much." She clapped her hands.

"Wait a minute," said Richard. "I haven't finished." He held up his soccer ball for everyone to see and then sat on it. "Male ostriches are very good fathers. They sit on the eggs all during the night, and the ugly females sit on them all day. You might know the poor fathers would get night shift."

Jed couldn't stop laughing. "Wait," he finally managed to say. "I really want to get a picture of this. Where's my camera?"

Richard rolled off the soccer ball and landed on his tail feathers. "It must be pretty hard for an ostrich to sit on ten eggs at a time. Those ugly, scrawny females probably can't do it." He tried to climb back on the ball.

Gina reached for the soccer ball and threw it toward the edge of the yard. It bounced down the ravine and into the creek. "Hey, my egg!" yelled Richard.

"Thank you very much for an excellent bird talk," said Gina, rolling her eyes upward. "We all enjoyed it a lot, didn't we?"

"I can't believe you gave this talk in science class," said Carrie.

Gina clapped her hands and turned to Carrie and Jed. Jed was gone.

"Where'd Jed go?" she asked.

"He went to get his camera," said Carrie.

"Back to the cabin? I told him no cameras are allowed—" Gina stopped when she saw Jed burst out of the woods, completely out of breath. He leaned against the birch tree and tried to control his wobbling knees.

"What's the matter?" asked Richard.

"I just . . . I just saw something."

"What?"

"I saw a dead body. I tripped on it. Fell flat on my face."

"Slow down, Jed," said Gina. "What happened?"

"I took a shortcut to the cabin so I could get my camera, and there it was."

"What?" asked Richard.

"A dead body. Come on, I'll show you."

"No thanks," said Carrie, backing away from Jed.

"We'd better take a look," said Gina. "Maybe it's the person who took the doll."

"Show it to us," said Richard.

Jed cautiously led the way into the woods, followed by

Gina. Carrie trailed reluctantly, her hands covering her entire face, with slits between her fingers to see through. Clyde padded silently beside Carrie. Richard brought up the rear, his headdress tied around his waist. The feathers bounced up and down behind him as he crept along on tiptoe.

6

A MYSTERIOUS MESSAGE

"Shhh! You all sound like a herd of buffalo," said Gina. "Quiet down. Don't anyone step on a twig."

"I'm trying not to step on the dead body," said Jed. "If my calculations are correct, it ought to be right here."

"Don't wake the dead," whispered Richard. He stepped on a fallen branch, which cracked in two under his weight.

Carrie turned around just as Richard was about to tickle her. "Don't pull anything funny, Richard. Just stay behind me, all right?"

Richard straightened up. "Of course. I wasn't going to do anything. Would I do anything?"

They circled the cabin and explored three separate paths, but they found nothing. "This is a wild goose chase," said Gina. "There's no dead body out here. You're seeing things again, Jed."

"I saw a dead body," said Jed, scratching his head. "I *know* I did."

"Wait a minute," called Richard. "Look at that." He pointed to a piece of white paper tacked to the cabin door.

They all rushed up the porch steps and read the note that had been posted beside Gina's PRIVATE PROPERTY sign. The note said:

IF YOU WANT DOLL, MEET ME HERE TONIGHT

"Who wrote this?" asked Richard.

"Maybe that dead body wasn't dead after all," said Jed.

Gina studied the crooked lettering on the paper. "Strange. Tiffany can't write like this. I must have been wrong about her taking the doll." She felt suddenly ashamed of the way she had suspected her sister.

"I know who wrote this," whispered Carrie. "It was the ghost. Sophie Owens's ghost. She's come back to her childhood home. I told you so. Ohhh, let's go."

"There's no ghost," insisted Gina. "Somebody is playing a trick on us. And it's not funny."

The campers opened the cabin door and walked inside. "I don't care if this is Camp Kickapoo, I'm getting my binoculars," said Richard. "Maybe I'll be able to see who's prowling around here."

Gina hesitated but finally led the way upstairs to the girls' pile of sleeping bags and suitcases. "I put them here," she said and then stopped. "They're gone!" She searched all around her sleeping bag.

"Are you sure?" asked Richard.

"I'm positive. I put them on my sleeping bag."

"Where's my camera?" asked Jed.

Gina opened her suitcase. Jed's camera lay on top of her clothes. She reached into the suitcase pocket. "Your watch is still here," she said as she pulled Carrie's watch from the pocket.

Jed hung the camera strap around his neck. "No one is getting my camera."

Carrie took the watch from Gina and fastened it around her wrist. "At least the ghost didn't find this."

"First the doll and now my binoculars," said Richard. "This is getting serious. I want my binoculars back."

The four campers descended the stairs and stepped out into the speckled sunlight of the woods. Discussing the mysterious note and the missing binoculars, they made their way back to Gina's yard.

The screen door opened as John came outside carrying a plateful of hamburgers. He turned on the gas grill.

Gina motioned to her campers to stay quiet. If John knew about the note on the cabin door, Camp Kickapoo would be over for sure. Her father whistled merrily as he placed the hamburgers on the grill. Gina pulled everyone toward her until all four heads met over the sundial in a tight huddle.

"Okay, here's the plan," she whispered. "Tonight, we're all staying in the cabin. All four of us. A guard for each window."

"That's what you think," said Carrie.

"Shhh." Gina smiled at her father and then pressed her head again into the huddle. "We have to get that doll for

Grandma. And whoever took it probably has Richard's binoculars too. So tonight we wait in the cabin and catch the culprit."

"Awesome," said Richard.

"But, Gina, I'm scared," whispered Carrie.

"Listen, with all four of us, we'll get the doll back with no problem. Four to one. Are you with me?"

"By my calculations, there will be four kids to one ghost," said Jed. "I don't like those numbers at all."

Gina spoke with sudden certainty. "Someone's playing a terrible trick, and tonight we find out who. Don't you want to find out who stole our doll?"

"And my binoculars," added Richard.

"What's everyone whispering about?" asked John. The campers jumped when they heard his deep voice.

"Oh, nothing, nothing at all," said Gina. "Just making plans." She pointed to the sundial and pretended to be intensely interested in figuring out the time. John nodded and turned back to his hamburgers.

"This could be the biggest adventure of our lives," she whispered.

"Chances are good it'll be the last adventure of our lives," said Jed.

"I wouldn't miss it for anything," said Richard. "Count me in."

"Me too," Jed said quickly before he could change his mind.

"Ohhhh." Carrie closed her eyes and moaned. "How do I get into these things?"

"Good!" Gina thrust out her hand for everyone to slap, and it was smacked hard by Richard, then Jed, and finally by Carrie.

"All for one, and one for all," said Gina. "We help fellow Kickapoos at all times." They all joined in the chant.

"Anyone hungry?" called Gina's mother from the patio. She spread a red-and-white-checked tablecloth on the picnic table. She was followed by Grandma, who carried a large salad bowl. Tiffany brought out a bag of hamburger buns and a jar of catsup.

"I've got plenty of hamburgers," called John to the Kickapoo campers. "Anyone want a big, juicy hamburger smothered with cheese and onions and tomatoes and catsup and pickles and—"

"No thanks," called Gina. "We don't eat hamburgers. We're pioneers. We made our own bread." She walked over to the rock by the shed, picked up a dried bread blob, and tasted it.

"Did I say hamburgers?" said her father. "These are really buffaloburgers. Just like pioneers used to eat."

"Buffaloburgers!" cried Richard. "That's different. Pioneers love buffaloburgers." He and Jed ran to the table and slid into a spot on the bench, next to Tiffany.

"I guess we could have buffaloburgers with our bread," said Gina as she scraped the loaves from the rock and came to the table with Carrie. "I had planned on snail sandwiches, but we could have those tomorrow night." She passed the loaves around to the other three campers and gave the smallest one to Tiffany.

71

"Snail sandwiches," said Jed. "Gee, that would have been scrumptious. We'll just have to wait 'til tomorrow for that treat."

"Where's Dwayne?" asked Gina.

"Reading. He's in the middle of a book he cannot put down," said Gina's mother. "He'll be out later."

As soon as John said grace, Tiffany bit into her bread. "Blah! This tastes like cardboard."

"You are not a true pioneer." Gina chewed her bread and swallowed it. "Not bad."

Richard, Jed, and Carrie bit into their bread and smiled weakly. "I think I broke a tooth," said Richard.

"So tonight's the big camp-out, huh, Gina?" said John.

"Yeah, we're all set."

"Did you find my doll?" Grandma asked. Her face was so full of hope that it nearly broke Gina's heart to tell her that the doll was still missing.

"But don't worry, Grandma. We're going to find it tonight for sure," promised Gina.

"It has been so many years, but I can still remember that doll," said Grandma.

Grandma told Gina's parents all about the doll and how it came to be buried. "I don't understand," said Gina's father. "A doll can't disappear like that. It must be here somewhere."

"Don't worry, we'll find it tonight," said Gina.

"I didn't lose it," said Tiffany. "Somebody took it."

Gina looked at Tiffany. "I think you're right, Tiffany."

"Don't you want to come back to Camp Kickapoo?" Carrie asked Tiffany.

"No." Tiffany bit off the end of a celery stick and frowned as she chewed. She wouldn't look at Gina. "I have to call Sarah. I want her to come and visit me," she told Carrie.

The campers enjoyed their buffaloburgers and ate some baked beans and salad too. They carried their dishes and cups into the kitchen. Dwayne looked up from his book. "Still having your camp?" he asked.

"Yeah," said Gina.

"How long does this camp of yours last?"

"I don't know. Maybe a month." Dwayne nodded and returned to his reading.

"Can't we use flashlights?" asked Carrie as the Kickapoo campers walked to the shed beside the garage. "It's going to be dark in that cabin tonight. Real dark."

"No flashlights," said Gina. "Those were invented after 1800. We're going to make lightning bug lanterns." She passed around four canning jars. The campers scurried from one yard to the next catching lightning bugs and putting them into the jars. The bugs glowed on and off.

After the boys pulled their bags and blankets from inside the tent, the campers made their way into the woods. "I wish these lanterns would light up a little more often," said Carrie. "I can't see a thing." She cried out and almost dropped her jar as a furry animal brushed against her leg and leaped onto a nearby tree. She held her lantern high over her head with a trembling hand.

"What is it?" asked Gina. She peered into the darkness. Two shiny eyes stared down at her from a low-hanging branch.

73

"It's Clyde, that's all. Just Clyde," said Carrie. "Go home, Clyde. Shoo!"

The moon came out from behind a cloud, lighting a portion of the path in front of them. Jed jumped back. "Yow! There's the dead body!"

Everyone scrambled back and then inched forward again. "Where? I don't see it," said Richard.

"Gosh, are you blind?" Jed pointed to a large boot that protruded from under a rotting log.

"Is that it?" asked Gina.

"Right there under the log. See?" said Jed. "The tree must have fallen on him."

"Ohhh, how awful!" wailed Carrie.

"Who is it?" asked Gina.

Richard dropped his suitcase and walked over to the boot just as the moon vanished behind another cloud, leaving them in darkness. He reached over and pulled the boot loose.

"He pulled off his leg!" screamed Carrie. "Aaagh!"

"Pipe down. It's nothing but an old boot." Richard tossed the boot at Carrie's feet, and she shrieked again.

Jed pulled a flashlight from his back pocket and pointed a beam of light back and forth across the path, illuminating the log and the boot. "You can keep your lightning bug lanterns," he said, "but I'm using my flashlight." He set his jar on the ground, unscrewed the lid, and released his lightning bugs.

Gina said nothing. She was secretly thankful for the flashlight, modern or not, and continued the march toward the cabin. The dark house loomed ahead in the shadows. No one spoke a word until they reached the porch.

"Who's going in first?" asked Jed.

"Gina is. Camp directors always get to go first," said Richard as he pushed Gina up the steps.

"Thanks," said Gina. She turned the doorknob, but the door was locked. "Who locked the door?"

"Not me," came the response from everyone behind her.

Gina thought back to the moment when she, Carrie, and Tiffany had left the cabin earlier that day. "Tiffany must have pressed the button on the lock when we left this afternoon."

"Super," said Carrie. "So how do we get in?"

"I have a key, but I forgot and left it in my suitcase," said Gina. "We'll have to climb through a window." Richard and Jed dropped their gear on the porch. The four campers circled the cabin, trying to find an open window, but the windows were closed tight.

"There's an upstairs window that will open," said Jed. "Real easy."

"How do you know?" asked Gina.

"Because I climbed through it the other day," he answered. "All you have to do is climb that tree and jump onto the roof. Nothing to it."

With his flashlight, Jed sent a beam of light across the upstairs window. He handed the flashlight to Gina. "Here, you'll need this."

"Me? Why me?"

" 'Cause you're the camp director," said Jed.

"The camp director has to do everything," muttered Gina as she slipped the flashlight into her back pocket and climbed up the tree trunk and out onto the branch that hung over the roof. She dropped easily from the branch to the shingled roof. On hands and knees, she crawled to the window and was about to lift the sash when she noticed a dark object on the roof a few feet to her left. She reached for it and had barely touched it when the object slipped downward. Richard's binoculars. They tumbled to the edge of the roof and almost dropped out of sight.

Without a word, Gina crawled along the sloping porch roof. A shingle under her right knee broke loose, slid to the edge, and fell to the ground. Gina grabbed at the roof with her fingernails, almost losing her balance.

"What's going on?" asked Carrie.

"What's taking so long?" called Jed.

Gina snatched the binoculars, hung the strap around her neck, and pulled the flashlight from her pocket. She directed a beam of light across the roof but saw nothing else. Carefully, she climbed back to the window. The window slid up easily, and she clambered into the shadowy bedroom. Holding the flashlight in front of her like a weapon, she sent a weak beam of light from ceiling to floor. Needs new batteries, she thought.

And then another idea struck her. What if someone had locked the cabin door on purpose? What if someone was already inside the cabin, waiting for their arrival? She began to whistle a perky little tune as she walked quickly across the creaking floorboards. She tore down the stairs as

fast as she could and reached for the front doorknob. The lock clicked open as she twisted the knob.

"About time," grumbled Richard. "We thought you were baking a cake in here or something."

"Look what I found on the roof." Gina pulled the strap over her head and handed Richard his binoculars.

"Hey, my binoculars!"

"Almost killed myself getting them."

"They were on the roof?" asked Carrie.

"Yeah," said Gina.

"See anything else?" asked Carrie.

"No."

Carrie, Richard, and Jed tumbled on top of one another as they pushed into the cabin. Clyde yowled loudly as Jed shut the door on his tail.

"Oops, sorry, Clyde. I didn't see you."

Richard and Jed carried all of their equipment up the stairs and dumped it in the east bedroom, above the kitchen. Gina flashed her light around the two downstairs rooms and then climbed the steps behind the boys. Carrie was two inches behind her.

"I had this weird idea," said Gina when she reached the top of the stairs.

"You always have weird ideas," said Richard with a laugh.

"I was wondering if maybe whoever is going to meet us here tonight is already here, waiting for us."

Carrie gasped. "Where?" She grabbed Gina's arm.

"Let's check the closet." Everyone followed Gina as she

walked to the closet in the west bedroom and threw open the door. "No one here."

"If there was someone in here already, he'd have to be hiding in the attic," said Jed.

"What attic?" asked Gina.

Jed took the flashlight and directed it upward. "I was out here the other day, and I heard mice up in the attic. That's when I discovered this trapdoor." His beam of light stopped at a rectangular door set into a crude ceiling made of wide boards just above the rafters.

Gina ran to the other bedroom and brought back a chair. "Someone give me a boost. I want to see what's up there."

Jed and Gina climbed onto the chair while Carrie and Richard held it steady. Jed laced his fingers into a stirrup and hoisted Gina to the ceiling. She pushed open the trapdoor and pulled herself up into the crawl space. Richard tossed the flashlight to her, and she pointed the feeble light all around the space. She sucked in her breath as a mouse ran across her left hand.

"What's the matter?" yelled Carrie.

"Mice," said Gina as she dropped back into the bedroom. "Nothing up there but a couple hundred mice. Where's Clyde?"

"I hate mice," said Carrie. "I hate this cabin. I hate this whole camping trip."

Gina dusted herself off and looked around. "I guess we're going to have to wait. Each one of us gets a window to guard. Between us, we ought to be able to see anything coming toward the cabin."

"I get it," said Richard. "The first person to spot something weird has to signal everyone else."

"Exactly," said Gina.

"What's the signal?" asked Jed.

"Hoot like an owl," said Gina.

Richard decided to practice a few hoots and was getting warmed up when the front door squeaked open on its rusty hinges. Richard's mouth was still shaped like an O, but nothing came out.

"Didn't you lock the door?" Gina whispered to Carrie.

"Me? Was I supposed to lock it?"

They listened intently as someone stepped into the cabin and closed the door. All was silent for several seconds until the quiet visitor began to climb the stairs.

THE KNOCK ON THE CABIN DOOR

Within seconds, the Kickapoo campers were blinded by a bright light. A tall person in the shadows aimed a flashlight beam into their faces. Gina backed up and fell over Richard's suitcase.

"I swear, it sounds like a barnful of hoot owls in here," said the voice behind the flashlight.

"Mom!" cried Carrie. Her mother lowered the flashlight to the floor and entered the room.

"How are the campers tonight?" she asked as she peered around the cabin. "Boy, this looks like a fun place for a camp-out."

"It is," said Jed.

"I tell you what, though, I'd be petrified of rats." Mrs. Carlton flashed her light into a corner.

"There aren't any rats," said Gina, "just a few little mice."

"Well, I came to get Tiffany's tiger. I was over visiting your mother, Gina, and I told her I'd come and get Tiffany's things for her. Tiffany says she can't sleep without her tiger."

Mrs. Carlton gathered up Tiffany's sleeping bag, her small suitcase, and the stuffed tiger. Still holding the flashlight, she made her way to the stairs. "Are you sure you're okay?"

"Oh, we're fine," said Gina.

"Tiffany tells me you lost that doll you dug up."

"It's gone," said Gina. "We don't know what happened to it."

"A real shame," said Mrs. Carlton. "Might be worth a whole lot of money. You let me know if it turns up. I'd give anything to see it."

"Oh, we will," said Gina.

"Bye, Mom," said Richard and Carrie.

All at once Clyde darted from a dark corner. "A rat!" Mrs. Carlton screamed, jumped a foot in the air, and began kicking her feet in every direction.

"It's only Clyde," shouted Gina.

The shrieking stopped. "Clyde? Oh, you naughty cat, you naughty, naughty cat." The campers tried to catch Clyde, but he leapt back into the rafters. Mrs. Carlton's shoes clicked down the steps and out the door.

"Okay, campers, it's time to take our stations. Everyone pick a window and remember, hoot like an owl if you see anybody coming," said Gina.

"Who do you think will come?" asked Carrie.

"Whoever took the doll. Whoever wrote that note," said Gina.

Before Richard took his place at his window, he felt his way down the stairs and bolted the door. He returned to the bedroom at the right of the stairway and knelt by a window. Jed sat by the other window.

Gina and Carrie waited quietly in the opposite bedroom and listened to the creakings of the house in the growing wind. "I'm sleepy," said Gina after several minutes had passed. "How 'bout you?"

"Me too. I don't think anyone is coming," said Carrie. She yawned.

"I think that note was a trick. Someone is just playing a mean trick on us."

They got up and walked to the boys' bedroom, only to find Richard and Jed fast asleep on the floor in front of their windows. "Some night watchmen they make," said Gina with a laugh.

The girls returned to the other room, took off their shoes, and crawled into their sleeping bags. "What time is it?" asked Gina.

Carrie looked at her glow-in-the-dark watch. "Midnight."

"I don't feel like a pioneer with all these modern conveniences," said Gina. "Watches. Flashlights."

"I don't care," said Carrie. "I'm glad we have them."

Gina opened her jar and released the lightning bugs she had caught. Then she opened Carrie's. "Go ahead. Fly away, lightning bugs."

At that moment, a tapping sounded on the cabin door. "Who's that?" whispered Carrie.

"I don't know."

"Well, aren't you going to answer it? Remember the note? It said MEET ME HERE TONIGHT," said Carrie. "This is it. Answer the door."

Gina's heart beat faster as the knocking on the door grew louder. "I don't want to." She scrunched down deeper into her sleeping bag. "You answer it. I bet it's your mom again. She probably forgot something. Go on."

"No way," said Carrie. "I wouldn't go down those stairs for all the money in the whole world."

They listened carefully but heard nothing more. "Did it go away, do you think?" asked Gina after a few minutes of silence.

"It's probably coming up the stairs," whispered Carrie. "Ghosts can go straight through doors, even locked ones, can't they?"

Gina didn't wait to answer. She jumped out of her sleeping bag and moved as noiselessly as she could toward the closet. By the time she reached the closet and opened the door, Carrie was behind her, pushing to get inside too. They pulled the closet door closed. Barely breathing, they listened for more sounds but heard nothing.

"Maybe we ought to hoot like an owl," whispered Gina, "to warn the boys."

"You do, and we're all dead."

"But what about—" Gina moved an inch to the right, and her bare foot came down on something squishy. She bent over and pulled the mushy substance from between her toes. Her hand touched something on the floor next to

her foot, something small and round and soft. "An eyeball," she whispered. "I just stepped on an eyeball. What's in this closet, anyway?"

She felt along the floor until her fingers touched something else, something large, wet, and spongy. "Brains!" she whispered. She picked up the wet mass and shoved it toward Carrie.

"Don't!" cried Carrie as she felt the dripping, cold blob touch her arm.

"Shhh! Just feel this. I swear there's a dead body in here," whispered Gina. "And this one is real."

Gina reached down one more time and felt along the baseboard of the closet. Her hand touched an unmistakable bone, about four inches long. She shuddered as she wiped her hands on her shirt over and over. "Let's get out of here," she said.

The two girls burst out of the closet, dove back into their sleeping bags, and pulled them high over their heads.

"Gina," said Carrie in a very small voice.

"What?"

"Remember that blood we saw on the floor the other day?"

"Yeah?"

"Do you think there's a murderer living here? Do you think that was him knocking on the door?"

"I don't know. I don't know why we ever came out here. I wish we'd never dug that latrine. I wish we'd never found that doll."

"Gina, I just thought where the murderer might be hiding," said Carrie.

"I don't want to know!"

"In the kitchen cabinets. He's probably waiting for us to fall asleep, and then he's going to climb out of the cabinets and come up to get us."

Gina's eyes flew open. "We forgot to check the cabinets. Oh, Carrie! We've got to go down and check."

"No way," said Carrie. "I'm not going anywhere."

Something clamped down heavily on Gina's head. "Help me, Carrie, help!" she screamed as it began to claw at her sleeping bag. The clawing continued for what seemed like hours as Gina scrunched down even lower in her bag. And then the heavy weight left as quickly as it had come, and she didn't hear a sound, except for the beating of her heart. And Richard's snoring.

Carrie laughed. Gina peeked out from her sleeping bag and found Carrie sitting beside her holding Clyde. Clyde began to purr. "It was only Clyde," said Carrie.

"Oh, Clyde!" Gina closed her eyes tight again and tried to sleep, but all she could think about was someone hiding in the kitchen cabinets. She thought about that until she fell asleep twenty minutes later.

The next morning, Gina awoke with a start as an eggshell cracked two feet above her and a raw egg dropped into her open mouth. "Bombs away!" yelled Richard. He and Jed slapped hands and whooped with laughter. "What a shot. I told you I could do it. Perfect hit."

"Man, I can't believe they never woke up," said Jed.

"Even when you tripped on the steps, they still never woke up."

"I thought they were dead. They look like zombies." Richard howled even louder.

"Look at Carrie's hair. Ha ha ha!" Jed messed Carrie's hair even more.

Gina coughed and spit out the slimy egg. It slid down her chin and onto her sleeping bag. "What are you trying to do, choke me to death?" She coughed some more and tried to wipe the slime from her sleeping bag. She scooped up some and threw it at Richard.

"Hey, is that nice?" Richard ducked as the egg splattered onto the wall. "Is that what I get for trying to bring you breakfast in bed? Delicious scrambled eggs. Yummy delicious scrambled—"

"I'll scramble you!" Gina leaped from her sleeping bag and tried to grab Richard, but as usual he was too fast.

"Is that appreciation, or what?" shouted Richard.

When Gina saw the closet door, she suddenly remembered the scare of the night before. "Richard, take a look inside that closet."

"Make me," said Richard.

"No, don't!" cried Carrie. "Don't open that door, whatever you do."

Richard quickly changed his mind. "I will if I want. You got a present for me in there?" He raced to the closet and swung open the door. Jed, Carrie, and Gina huddled behind him and peered over his shoulder. On the floor of the closet were several grapes, a cardboard box with the remains of two chicken drumsticks spilling out, a large sponge, and three small bottles of paint.

"Oh, boy, just what I always wanted," said Richard.

"Those weren't eyeballs," said Carrie. "Those were grapes."

Gina examined the closet carefully. "It sure looks to me like someone has been stashing their lunch in here. And what's all this paint stuff?"

"Remember those pictures we found yesterday, Gina?" said Carrie.

"And those blood spots," said Gina as she picked up a bottle of red paint. "That wasn't blood at all. It was paint."

"Ghosts don't eat grapes, do they?" asked Jed.

"There is no ghost," said Gina. "Someone knocked on the door last night after you were asleep. If it had been a ghost, it would have come right through the door, wouldn't it? Ghosts don't stand around knocking on doors, waiting for someone to open them."

"Who was it, then?" asked Jed.

"I don't know. We were too scared to open the door."

"Oh, brother. Too scared. That was our big chance to find out who's been stealing everything around here. You blew it," said Richard.

"Well, you were too busy snoring to answer the door," said Gina. They talked together as they made their way out of the cabin and back through the woods up the path to Gina's backyard.

Gina's mother and grandmother sat at the picnic table sipping coffee. They waved as the bedraggled campers entered the sun-warmed yard. "I've got corn fritters," Grandma told the campers as they walked up to the table. "Just like the pioneers ate."

"There are plenty inside," said Gina's mother. "Help yourselves."

"Thanks. That sounds great," said Gina. She ordered the campers to sit on the ground in a circle, Indian style, and then went inside to get some corn fritters.

"Why didn't you answer the door last night when John went out to check on you?" asked Gina's mother after Gina returned with a tray of food and plates.

Gina almost dropped the tray. "That was John?"

"He went out around midnight," said her mother, "but he said no one answered the door so he figured you were all sound asleep."

"He should have said something," said Gina. "We thought it was a . . . a burglar or something." She debated about telling her mother about the jars of paint they had found in the closet, and the bits and pieces of food. But it would only worry her, she knew, and maybe cause her to close the cabin for good, so Gina said nothing.

The screen door opened, and Tiffany and Dwayne came outside. Tiffany walked over to Gina and handed her an envelope.

"What's this?" Gina asked.

"It's got your name on the front," said Tiffany.

"Where'd you get this?" Gina took the envelope from Tiffany's hand.

"We heard a knock on the front door just a few minutes

ago. When we opened it, there was this envelope," Tiffany answered.

"Did you see anyone?" asked Richard.

"Didn't see anyone, did we, Dwayne?"

"Nope. Didn't see anyone," said Dwayne.

"Open the letter," said Tiffany. "Hurry up."

"I will, I will," said Gina. "After I eat my fritters." She bit into a warm fritter and watched as her mother and grandmother picked up their coffee cups and walked back inside. Dwayne followed behind, slamming the door as he went.

Tiffany sat down beside Gina and waited. Finally she said, "Aren't you done with your fritters yet?"

"Oh, okay," said Gina. She ripped open the envelope and read the note aloud to Carrie, Richard, Jed, and Tiffany:

STAY OUT OF MY HOUSE IF YOU VALUE YOUR LIFE

Nobody said a word as they all gazed at the crooked letters.

"This is a prank," said Gina. "I know this is a prank. Gosh, I wish you saw who put this envelope on the front porch."

"I didn't see anyone," said Tiffany. "No one. And Dwayne and I looked all around."

"Of course you didn't see anyone," said Carrie. "You can't see ghosts."

"Awesome!" said Richard. "A real live ghost!"

"A real dead ghost," said Jed.

"There's no such thing as ghosts," said Gina. "Some joker wrote this. Someone who likes to play games. And nobody is telling me to stay out of my cabin. That cabin is on my property, and I'll go in there anytime I feel like it."

"Yeah," said Tiffany. "Me too."

"Sophie Owens," said Carrie. "I knew it all along. She's never going to give back your grandmother's doll. We may as well give up. You can't fight a ghost."

"I'm not giving up," said Gina. "There's someone in the cabin who wants us out, and it isn't Sophie Owens. I bet whoever wrote these notes is in the cabin this very minute. And I bet the doll is there too."

"Let's go look," said Tiffany.

"Okay, let's go," agreed Gina. She jumped to her feet. "There's only one way to find out." She started toward the woods with Tiffany close behind her.

"I'm not going back there," said Carrie. "I'm afraid, Gina."

"Count me out too," said Richard. "It says STAY OUT OF MY HOUSE IF YOU VALUE YOUR LIFE. Sorry, but I value my life. Come on, Jed. Let's go to your house."

Jed didn't say anything. He glanced at Gina, turned, and followed Richard and Carrie out of the yard.

Gina watched her campers desert her, too stunned to respond. Finally, she hollered after them, "Wait a minute.

You can't walk away and leave me like this. We're supposed to help each other. All for one, and one for all." But Carrie, Jed, and Richard were gone. "Some brave pioneers. They leave me here all by myself."

"I'm here," piped up Tiffany.

Gina looked down at her sister and smiled. "I'm glad you're here. You're the bravest pioneer I've got." She shook her head. Strange that her little sister would stick with her, but her best friends chickened out just when she needed them. Maybe Tiffany was not so terrible after all.

"I'm not afraid," said Tiffany, but her small voice told Gina otherwise.

Gina grasped her sister's hand. "Come on, Tiffany."

They ran to the cabin. The two girls were startled by what they found when they entered the clearing. Sleeping bags, pillows, blankets, and suitcases were piled high on the cabin's porch. Someone had removed all their camping equipment and dumped it squarely outside the front door.

"Look!" Tiffany pointed to Gina's pillow. Smack in the middle lay a dead mouse.

"Ugh!" Gina picked up the mouse by the tail and tossed it to the ground. She rummaged through the rest of the camping gear, searching for the doll. But the doll was not there.

"We're going to find that doll," said Gina.

"You and me." Tiffany grinned up at Gina, but her smile suddenly faded.

"What's the matter?" Gina turned around, following Tiffany's frozen gaze to the second floor of the cabin.

"I saw someone."

"Where?" asked Gina.

Tiffany pointed to the bedroom window. "I saw someone at that window."

Gina studied the window but saw nothing. "I'm going inside."

"Me too."

"No, Tiffany, maybe you should stay out here," Gina said.

"If you're going in, I'm going with you. Please, Gina?"

"Oh, all right." Before she could reconsider, Gina reached for the doorknob, opened the door, and stepped inside. A bucket hanging above her tipped over and dumped greenish water onto her head. Tiffany jumped back onto the porch.

"Who's here?" cried Gina.

"GET OUT OF MY HOUSE!" called a voice from an upstairs room. The same strange thumping sound was heard approaching the stair landing.

"Gina!" Gina spun around. Carrie, Richard, and Jed rushed into the cabin clearing, out of breath. "Hey, Gina!" called Richard. "We came back to help you. You can't fight a ghost all by yourself. Just you and Tiffany."

"We changed our minds," said Carrie. "We're in this together."

"All for one, and one for all," said Jed.

Gina ran out onto the porch and slammed the front door behind her. "What happened to you?" asked Carrie when she saw Gina's dripping hair and wet shirt.

"Someone's in the cabin," said Gina in a low voice.

"Watch out!" said Tiffany. "Don't step on the mouse." Carrie, Richard, and Jed stepped around the mouse and climbed the porch steps.

"I'm going back in," said Gina. She reached for the doorknob again, but at that instant, she heard the lock click. She turned the doorknob, but the door would not open. She knew that whoever was in the cabin was standing on the other side of the door.

Without a word, Gina raced to the tree and began to climb. "Watch the windows." She shinned up the trunk of the tree, hopped onto the roof, and quickly crawled on hands and knees to the window. She raised the window, climbed inside, and then stood still, listening. This was Sophie's old house. Maybe Sophie had come back to her old home. Maybe Sophie had set up that bucket of water downstairs. Gina glanced upward. The trapdoor was open. A two-inch opening gaped between the door and the ceiling boards.

She walked across the room and stepped out onto the stairway landing. She noticed an easel set up in the west bedroom. Several jars of paint stood on the table, along with a tall stack of books. A sketch of a robin's nest with a mother bird and three baby birds hung on the easel.

Gina ran down the steps, two at a time, and opened the front door, standing aside as all the Kickapoo campers poured into the cabin. Tiffany came in last. They peered around, saying nothing, but searching every corner.

"No one came outside," said Carrie.

"Come with me," said Gina. She motioned for Richard to follow her upstairs. "The rest of you, check the kitchen."

Gina bounded back up the steps with Richard behind her. She strode across the west bedroom and threw open the closet door. Nothing.

It was after they checked the attic that Gina heard the strange bumping sound that she and Carrie had heard yesterday. "Listen! Do you hear that?" They both followed the noise back down the stairs.

Jed was in the kitchen poking the broom on the floor. "I checked all the cabinets," he said. "Nothing here."

"There's that bumping sound we heard," Gina told Carrie as she pointed to the broom.

"See anything upstairs?" asked Carrie.

Gina shook her head, frustrated. "We checked everywhere. The closet. The attic. No sign of anyone. No sign of the doll either."

"But I saw someone at the window," insisted Tiffany.

They all moved back into the main room, where they sat in a circle on the floor in front of the fireplace. "I give up," said Gina. "Whoever it is disappeared into thin air. Vanished like smoke."

"Vanished like a ghost, you mean," said Carrie. "Straight through the walls."

Gina pulled the note from her pocket.

STAY OUT OF MY HOUSE
IF YOU VALUE YOUR LIFE

She raised her arm over her head and shook the paper. "Okay, we'll leave. Do you hear me?" She directed her words to the ceiling. "You can keep your old house, Sophie. I don't want it. All I wanted was my grandmother's doll. That's all I wanted." She brushed the tears from her eyes.

Tiffany grabbed Gina's arm and pointed to the fireplace. Gina turned her head just in time to see a few black flakes fall from the chimney. Carrie, Richard, and Jed followed her gaze. Another bit of soot fell from the chimney onto the ashes below. It was then that Gina noticed the disturbance in the ashes, the clear prints of someone's feet.

Someone was hiding in the chimney.

8

FIREPLACE MYSTERY

"Look at me," said Gina, standing up. "I'm dripping wet. I guess I could at least build a fire and dry off before going home." She pointed to the chimney, winked, and held one finger to her lips in warning.

A puzzled expression crossed Carrie's face, but the others quickly realized that someone was inside the chimney. They played along.

"Yeah, a fire. Might as well," said Jed.

"Let's make a big one," said Tiffany.

"What can we use for paper?" asked Richard. "To get it started?"

"Run upstairs," said Gina. "Get that picture off the easel and any other paper you can find up there." She picked up a stick and began to push around pieces of charred wood in the fireplace.

"Be right back," yelled Richard.

No sooner were the words out of Richard's mouth when a soot-covered figure dropped clumsily to the fireplace below, knocking the stick from Gina's hand. She jumped back as Dwayne crawled out from his hiding place, cov-

ered from head to toe with ashes. His soot-streaked face startled everyone.

"Dwayne!" Gina's hands flew to her face in disbelief. Carrie ran to the door but then turned around.

After a moment of surprise, Tiffany began to laugh. Dwayne scowled as usual, but his dirty face struck her as extremely funny. She had never seen her brother so dirty.

"Leave my pictures alone!" shouted Dwayne as he rushed toward the stairway.

Richard hurried back down the stairs, holding his hands over his head. "I didn't touch them." He stared wide-eyed at Dwayne.

"That's your painting up there on the easel?" asked Gina.

"Yes, it's my painting. Don't ever touch my stuff again."

"When did I ever—" Gina stopped. She remembered the fire she and Carrie had built the day before. She remembered burning all the pictures she had found in the cabin. "So you're the artist!"

"Yeah, I am." Dwayne looked down at his dirty sneakers. "You destroyed a picture of my mother that I'd worked on for weeks. I don't want to forget what she looks like." He glanced up, and for the first time, Gina saw the pain in his eyes.

"I was so mad I just wanted you out of here," he continued. "I worked so long on that picture, and you burned it up in one minute."

No one said a word. Dwayne fumbled with his collar as he tried to explain. "I'm sorry I tried to scare you, but it was the only way I could think of to get you out of here. I thought I'd found the perfect place to hide, to get away from all the noise. To get away from everything."

"You're the ghost!" said Carrie. She pointed her finger at Dwayne as she walked back into the room. "*You're* the one who said 'Get out of my house.' It wasn't Sophie Owens at all."

"We thought there was a real ghost out here," said Jed.

"That's what I was hoping you'd think," said Dwayne. "Then you'd get scared and leave me alone. I like it here. I had my own private place until your camp got started." He looked directly at Gina. "Your radio drives me nuts. And the TV's going all day long. I can't think in the house. I can't read. I can't paint. I can't do anything."

"Did you take Grandma's doll?" asked Gina.

Dwayne rubbed his chin, streaking it with soot. "Well, yeah, I did," he said with a sheepish expression on his face. "I figured you'd get out of here fast if you lost your doll and thought a ghost took it." A small smile pulled at his mouth, the first Gina could remember seeing. "I thought it was your doll. I didn't know it was Grandma's until I heard her talking about it this morning."

"Where is it?" asked Gina.

Dwayne hesitated. "I was going to give it back real soon. After you were good and scared." He shrugged his shoulders, defeated. "Oh well, what's the use? It's in my room, in my bottom dresser drawer."

"Did you take my binoculars too?" asked Richard.

"Yeah, I needed them for a picture I'm painting. I couldn't get close enough to the robin's nest, so I climbed

101

out on the porch and used the binoculars to see better. Didn't I put them back with your stuff?"

"No," said Gina. "I found them on the roof."

"Those binoculars weren't yours to take," said Richard. "You should have asked me first."

"I was afraid you wouldn't let me use them, and anyway, I couldn't let you know that I was painting out here. I was going to put them back as soon as I finished my picture," said Dwayne.

Richard frowned at Dwayne's excuses. Dwayne shouldn't have taken his binoculars, no matter what the reason was.

"Did you come out here last night?" asked Carrie.

"I was going to," answered Dwayne, "but I never made it. I was planning on giving you the biggest scare of your life so you'd think this place was haunted for sure, and never, ever, come back."

"Why didn't you?" asked Gina.

"I fell asleep reading and didn't wake up 'til morning. Blew my whole plan."

"Good thing," said Carrie. "We were plenty scared as it was."

"I don't get it," said Jed. "Who left the envelope on your front porch this morning?"

"I did," answered Dwayne. "I knocked on the wall behind the sofa to make Tiffany think someone was knocking on the door." He broke into a grin when he saw the exasperated look on Tiffany's face. "You fall for that trick every time."

Tiffany punched her brother playfully. "You're not very nice, Dwayne. You trick me all the time like that." He grabbed her hands and held them.

Gina felt a strange twinge of envy as she watched Tiffany and Dwayne. Tiffany was accustomed to Dwayne's tricks. Tiffany knew her brother as well as she knew the contents of her secret suitcase. Gina didn't know Dwayne at all. But then she had never really tried to know him, or understand him, or talk to him. And now he was her brother too.

It was all so different. She decided Grandma was right. She was going to have to do a lot of things differently. She would start by turning down her radio.

"Grandma!" said Gina. "Tomorrow's her birthday, and now we have a birthday present for her—her doll."

"Let's get it," said Carrie.

Gina started for the door and then looked back at Dwayne. "You didn't have to dump water all over me." She looked at her soiled shirt. "What'd you put in that water? Spinach? I'm turning green."

"Just a little green paint," said Dwayne.

"Wonderful."

"I'm sorry. I really am." He hesitated. "Wait a minute. I might as well give it to you now." He ran upstairs and returned with the picture of the robins in the nest. "Here. I made this one for you. Thought you might like it." He handed the picture to Gina.

Everyone crowded around for a good look at Dwayne's artwork. "Not bad," said Richard.

"It's good," said Carrie. "I like it."

Gina gazed at the picture for several moments. "I like it too. Thanks!"

A smile spread slowly across Dwayne's face. He wiped his sooty hand on his pants, reached out, and shook Gina's hand. "I'm glad you like it. I was afraid you wouldn't."

"I think it's beautiful," said Gina. She decided then and there to hang the picture in a special place in her bedroom.

"Come on, let's go," said Jed.

Gina carefully rolled the picture and tucked it under her arm. "Okay, everybody, time for our morning shower. Are you all ready?"

"Ready!" they shouted. The Kickapoo campers gathered their equipment and carried everything back to the tent in the backyard, leaving Dwayne by himself in the cabin.

"How come he gets the cabin?" grumbled Jed. "Who does he think he is?"

"That's all right," said Richard. "I like the tent better anyway."

"He was using the cabin first," said Gina. "Let's let him have it for a while. We'll get our turn someday. Don't worry."

"You mean we have to sleep in the tent tonight?" asked Carrie. "Richard snores!"

"I do not."

"You do too."

"You snore like a bear."

"Come on," said Gina. "Let's get the doll." They entered Gina's house and climbed the stairway to Dwayne's bedroom. In the bottom dresser drawer, just as Dwayne had said, Gina found the doll. She gave it to Tiffany to hold.

"Don't tell Grandma where we found it," said Gina.

"Why not?" asked Tiffany.

"I don't want her to know who took it, that's all."

"Why not?"

"Just because."

They quickly left Dwayne's room, walked down the hall, and entered Gina and Tiffany's room. They were startled to see Grandma sitting in a chair by the window. She was busy sewing the torn hem of the curtain.

Gina decided to give Grandma her present, even though it was one day early. "Happy birthday."

"Thank you, sweetheart, but it's not 'til tomorrow. Don't make me any older than I am."

"I know," said Gina, "but we have a special present for you right now. Look!" Gina motioned to Tiffany. Her sister drew the doll from behind her back and held it out to Grandma.

"Well, well, well," said Grandma as she took the doll into her arms. She gazed at her old toy, enrapt, almost as if sixty years had never passed. "She's beautiful, isn't she?"

"Oh, yes. She is!" agreed all the campers at once.

"Will you let me play with her?" asked Tiffany. "Please?"

"Tiffany," scolded Gina. "This is a very special doll, not to be played with."

But Grandma pulled Tiffany to her and let her hold the doll once again. "That's what dolls are for, to be played with. Just be careful with her."

"Come on, how about our camp?" said Richard. "Let's go hunt fossils down by the creek."

Gina hugged her grandmother. "Happy birthday, one day early, Grandma."

"Thank you, Gina. It's the very best present ever." Grandma's eyes twinkled with pleasure. "Would you answer one question before you go?"

"Sure."

"Whatever happened to your hair?"

Gina had forgotten all about her drenched hair and shirt. "Oh, I just had a little water spilled on me. That's all." She unfurled Dwayne's picture and showed it to her grandmother. "I got a present too. From Dwayne." Her grandmother beamed, genuinely pleased with Gina's gift as well as her own.

A few minutes later, after the Kickapoo campers had changed into swimming suits, Gina turned on the faucet and picked up the garden hose. "This may be Camp Kickapoo, but I think that just once, we'll use something modern. You all need a good shower. Line up."

Richard, Jed, Carrie, and Tiffany formed a straight line, which quickly fell apart as Gina shot ice cold water on them. She swept the hose left and right, spraying a long stream of water up and down the line. "Yow! That's cold!" cried Jed. He held his arms out in front to stop the spray. "Turn it off!"

"You're not clean yet," hollered Gina. Carrie tried to run away, but Gina chased her down with the hose.

Dwayne walked into the yard. Gina took one look at him, covered as he was with soot, and decided that he needed a shower more than anyone. She hit him with a blast of water. She thought he would run away and was surprised when he whooped and hollered like the rest of them until Richard wrenched the hose out of her hands and turned it on her.

"Stop it! Not me!" yelled Gina. "I'm the camp director."

"Camp directors need showers too," said Richard, spraying Gina's face.

When the shower was over, they fell onto the grass, exhausted. Dwayne walked quickly toward the back door. It was then that Gina noticed the empty tent.

"Hey, where's all our stuff?" she asked.

Dwayne turned around. "It's all in the cabin. I carried everything back."

"Huh? I thought you wanted us out of there," said Gina.

"I did," said Dwayne. "But I got to thinking about it, you know? Why don't you take the cabin half the week, and I'll have it the other half? What do you think?"

The Kickapoo campers exchanged glances. "That's a fair deal," said Carrie.

"So it's our turn now, right?" said Richard.

"Yeah, it's all yours."

"Do you want to be in our camp?" asked Gina. "We're hunting for fossils this morning, and after lunch, we're making a campfire and singing songs."

"We're having snail sandwiches for lunch," said Jed.

Dwayne shrugged his shoulders. "Yeah, maybe. I don't know. I'll think about it." Gina could tell he was pleased with the invitation, despite his lack of enthusiasm. She was glad she had asked him. Dwayne turned around and walked down the driveway.

"Why isn't Dwayne coming to camp?" asked Tiffany.

"He probably doesn't like snail sandwiches," said Carrie.

"Time to hunt for fossils," said Richard. "Let's change into dry clothes and meet down by the creek."

"Race you to the cabin," yelled Jed. The two boys sprinted across the yard and into the woods.

"There go the THINGS," said Carrie. Gina laughed. She knew that no matter how much Carrie complained about her brother, the two of them were still good friends. And if Carrie could get along with someone as crazy as Richard, she could easily live with Dwayne and Tiffany. And they could live with her.

"What's a fossil?" asked Tiffany.

"Something very old," said Gina.

"How old?" asked Tiffany. "Older than Grandma's doll?"

"Come on. I'll show you." She took Tiffany's hand, and the three girls ran down the lawn and into the woods.

ABOUT THE AUTHOR

LINDA GONDOSCH planned to be a writer when she was growing up in Cleveland, Ohio, and even founded a story-telling club for neighborhood children that met on her front porch. She taught high-school English briefly before devoting herself full-time to writing when her own four children started to reach school age. One of them, Lisa, held a summer camp in their backyard that inspired the story *Camp Kickapoo*.

Linda Gondosch has published many beloved books for young people, the first of which won the Kentucky Bluegrass Children's Choice Award. She now lives in Lawrenceburg, Indiana, with her husband, a civil engineer, and enjoys speaking at schools around the country.

PATRICIA HENDERSON LINCOLN, who has illustrated many books for children, lives in Longmeadow, Massachusetts.

The Midnight Society has a scary
new story to tell. . .

A brand new thriller series based on the hit
Nickelodeon® show!

THE TALE OF THE
SINISTER STATUES
by **John Peel**

THE TALE OF
CUTTER'S TREASURE
by **David L. Seidman**

THE TALE OF
THE RESTLESS HOUSE
by **John Peel**

A new title every other month!!

 A MINSTREL® BOOK

Published by Pocket Books

1053-03

Don't miss any of the adventure!

FRIGHTMARES™

Whenever pets–and their owners–get into trouble, Rosie Saunders
and Kayo Benton always seem to be in the middle of the action.
Ever since they started the Care Club ("We Care About Animals"),
they've discovered a world of mysteries and surprises. . .and danger!

CAT BURGLAR ON THE PROWL

BONE BREATH AND THE VANDALS

DON'T GO NEAR MRS. TALLIE
(coming in mid-July 1995)

By Peg Kehret

A MINSTREL® BOOK

Published by Pocket Books

1049-01

Award-winning author
Patricia Hermes brings you:

THE COUSINS' CLUB SERIES

#1: I'LL PULVERIZE YOU, WILLIAM

Summer will never be the same for the Cousins' Club...both creepy cousin William and an out-of-control boa constrictor have slithered into their vacation plans!

#2: EVERYTHING STINKS

Just one perfect day of fun—that's all that everyone in the Cousins' Club wants. But then one incredible event changes their very idea of perfect....

#3: THIRTEEN THINGS NOT TO TELL A PARENT

There are all kinds of ways to have a great summer. And most of them are going to get the Cousins' Club in big trouble!

Available from

A MINSTREL® BOOK

Published by Pocket Books

1097-02